MW00779643

FATAL, BUT FESTIVE

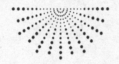

MAGGIE SHAYNE

Published by Oliver-Heber Books

0 9 8 7 6 5 4 3 2 1

❀ Created with Vellum

CHAPTER ONE

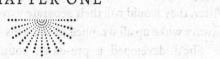

Kiley's House

*K*iley sat on her sofa in her living room for the first time in weeks and told herself this was what she'd wanted.

She'd never intended to stay at Jack's place for longer than it took the cops to finish digging up bodies from her basement and back yard. That was done. And the basement's concrete floor had been repaired, the secret prison beneath it, filled in. Her lawn was covered in a fresh carpet of grass. And the ghosts who'd scared the living hell out of her had all found peace and moved on to the other side.

She hoped.

She loved her house, even if it was the kind of place where you'd want to film a horror movie. That was part of its appeal. Kind of a way to thumb her nose at the ghosts who allegedly haunted the rural New York town of Burnt Hills and the psychics, channels, and readers who cashed in on them.

But then she'd found out they were real. And now here she was, back home in her big, spooky-AF house all by herself. She

1

liked her space. She'd been eager to get it back, after a month-and-a-half staying with Jack in his cramped little place.

He'd made up a tiny bedroom for her in his log cabin, but they'd shared his bed since Halloween. Every night. Which was weird, because their relationship was new. They didn't have sex every night, of course, though they did more often than not. After, they would roll their separate ways and go to sleep. But she always woke up all wrapped in his arms.

She'd developed a pre-dawn routine ninja-like moves to extract herself without waking him, so he wouldn't be embarrassed. Or maybe so she wouldn't. They hadn't really reached the wake-up-in-each-other's-arms-and-snuggle phase. They'd been best enemies only weeks ago. It was weird.

She'd been eager to get back into her place before Christmas. Her gorgeous old house with its turrets and widow's walk was full of gaudy holiday potential.

Maybe once she decorated, it wouldn't feel so lonely. She just couldn't seem to work up the enthusiasm to get started.

Some wind-driven piece of something hit the side of the house and she jumped so hard she sloshed wine onto her hand. At that precise moment, the old-fashioned twist-and-ring door-bell gave its shrill alarm and her heart stopped.

But when insistent knocking followed along with muffled shouts, she realized there was a human at her door—a living one —and went to open up.

Maya, Johnny, and Chris were huddled on her porch, all of them carrying stuff and being buffeted by the wind. "Well, what is all this?" She moved aside and held the door with her arm to let them in, but she wasn't looking at them. She was looking past them, a little bit embarrassed by the surge of joy she felt when Jack pulled in behind them, got out of his car, and came running, box under one arm, coat over his head.

He came in and kissed her—longer than a peck, but nothing passionate—and said, "Happy first night back."

Then he moved the box between them. "I brought cake."

"And I brought my veggie noodle soup!" Maya said, kind of hefting her crockpot a little higher on the way through to the kitchen. "The place looks great!" She was the oldest among them, a forty-something modern witch with shoulder length hair in that shade that might be platinum blond or white.

Chris had a gallon jug in either hand. "My grandma's rum punch. She made it every Christmas. Kicks like a mule. But it needs ice." He followed Maya into the kitchen.

Johnny looked from Kiley to Jack and back again, and then he just headed for the kitchen, too. Kiley handed him the cake box on the way by.

"It's uncanny, how much he resembles John, isn't it?" It wasn't the first time Kiley had made the observation. John Redhawk, their friend and resident shaman, had moved west to be closer to his daughter. But before he'd gone, he'd pitched his grandson to take his place in their little group of ghost... not busters. More like helpers.

John said his grandson had been touched by the gods. He had the gift, and years of training at his grandad's feet.

"Miss me yet?" Jack asked, drawing her attention away from the newest member.

"I've only been back here for twelve hours, Jack."

"So that's a yes then?"

"Yeah." He was neat, she was messy. He was an early riser, she liked to sleep in. He liked actual food, she liked garbage. And honestly, they both liked their space.

"Still think we're doing the right thing? Taking it slow?"

"Yeah," she replied without looking him in the eye.

He made an ouchie face, so she went on. "We've been dating for seven weeks. I think that's way too soon to move in. Besides, this is my dream house."

"Nightmare house."

"That's over. I love it here. There's so much room."

3

"There's room for a football team. But it still creeps me out."

"And you like being near The Magic Shop." His cabin was within two minutes of his new age tourist attraction. Readings in the back, by appointment only.

"We did okay, though, right?" he asked. "Living together?"

"Yes, because we both knew it was temporary. I didn't need to settle in. You didn't need to truly share your space. And remember what we talked about. Don't let all this—" she waved a hand at the dining room table where food was piling up. "Make you forget what I said. My place is *not* going to become spook central."

Somebody tapped on the door. Kiley frowned and said, "What now?"

And Jack said, "Nothing good," and he had that look on his face, half-acceptance and half-dread. He only got that look when there was a dead person nearby.

Kiley braced herself and went to opened the door.

There was a large red parka, hood pulled up, face hidden deep within. Short, though, and the hand clutching the collar beneath the chin was a female hand, bearing several rings. The ice storm, sleet and freezing rain, had intensified. The poor thing might've gone off the road or something.

"Can I help you?"

The visitor dropped like a sack of laundry.

"Holy–" Kiley bent, Jack crouching right alongside her..

"Here, let me," he said, and handed her a phone. Then he slid his arms underneath the fallen visitor while Kiley tapped 911, and then he straightened and turned toward her with only the empty coat in his arms.

"Nine-one-one, what's your emergency?"

Kiley looked from Jack's stunned face, to the parka he held, to the empty front step where the woman had been standing.

"Hello? What's your emergency? Can you speak?"

"No. I mean, yes. I mean, I called by accident. Sorry." She

disconnected as her other three guests returned from the kitchen, laughing and chatting until they saw the two of them standing there with the door wide open and an ice storm raging outside, gaping at an empty coat.

"Why do I get the feeling we just missed something big?" Maya rubbed her arms, then hurried past them to close the door. As soon as it closed, she stood very still, looking around. "Somebody was here."

"No *body* was here." Jack looked at each of them and said, "There was someone in this coat, and then there wasn't."

Kiley grabbed the coat from him and held it up by its fur trimmed hood. "Why my house? Huh? Why don't you dead people find some other house to haunt? *He's* the not-so-phony-after-all-psychic-channel-whatever! Why aren't you haunting *his* place?"

"Yeah, you dumb ghost." Jack gave a proud nod that Kiley read as, "See how supportive I am?" And took the coat back from her. Maya turned the lock on the door.

Johnny said, "Grandpa says energy finds its own way." He spoke in a slow, deep voice that could give you a boost of confidence or a shiver of fear. He didn't say a lot. Hadn't even told them what sort of ... abilities or whatever, he had. His grandfather said he was gifted, but he hadn't said how.

"What do you mean, it finds its own way?" Kiley asked and it came out a little snappy. "Why can't it find its own way somewhere else?"

"For the same reason a magnet clings to metal, and not to a tree or a stone."

She blinked slowly as her brain tried to put all that into muggle terms.

"Could be something about the location," Maya said. She was standing beside the door, near a tall window, holding its curtain aside to gaze out into the darkness and slashing sleet.

"Location?" Kiley asked.

Johnny tipped his head sideways. "If you say it's built on an ancient Indian burial ground, I swear—"

"I wouldn't say that any more than I would suggest it's been cursed by a Witch. "Her comeback was quick and dead on target, but delivered with a twinkle in her eyes that dulled its sharpest edge.

"It was a serial killer's torture chamber and burial ground," Kiley said. "That's plenty all by itself."

Maya nodded, then moved toward the dining table, which was already piled with dishes and food. Jack's cake, from Kiley's favorite bakery, sat beside the inner part of Maya's crockpot and a loaf of sliced brown bread that smelled like cinnamon.

Jack dropped the coat over the back of the sofa on the way back to the table.

Everyone sat and began filling their soup bowls. Chris, who'd been quiet and clearly deep in thought, finally said, "Maybe it's the fact that we're all here, the five of us, together."

Kiley gave him an eye roll and helped herself to a slice of the bread, which sne sniffed. "Banana?"

"Banana zucchini," Maya said.

Chris went on. "But this is what we wanted, right? To work together to help people not be scammed by phonies and help the dead if they need it, like we did for Miller's victims."

"Yes," Kiley said. "We all agreed to do this...but headquarters is back at Jack's shop, not in my dining room."

Word had got out about them. Burnt Hills was already a new-age sort of town, but finding the bodies of murder victims and rumors about their ghosts haunting this place had got out. Everyone whispered that the town's handful of genuinely gifted individuals among a vocation rife with frauds, had come together to solve a mystery. Emails and letters had been showing up in Kiley's inbox and at Jack's shop ever since.

"It might be nice to have an *actual* ghost to deal with," Chris said between bites of soup with broth so thick and veggies so dense it was more like a stew. "Instead of people with overactive imaginations and hints of paranoia."

"We always tell them the truth," Jack said. "And when they ask us to clear their houses anyway and we do it and the problem disappears, I believe we've helped them psychologically, even if the ghost wasn't real."

"Who's to say what's real?" Johnny asked. "What's real to one person is very different from what is real to another."

"Reality is a construct of the mind," Chris said, tapping his head amid its forest of longish dreads. Then he slathered a slice of the bread in butter, ate it in two bites, got up and carried his napkin with him into the living room. They watched him through the wide doorway that had once held double doors in it as he wiped his hands carefully, then picked up the coat and looked it all over.

"I think it's vintage. But it looks brand new." He frowned, looking at the tag inside the collar. "JaVoe," he said, then he spelled it out for them.

Jack pulled out his phone and started tapping while Chris went through the coat's pockets. The rest of them watched and kept on eating. Maya's cooking skills, Kiley had learned in the seven weeks they'd been working together, were not to be taken lightly. And her meals somehow *felt* as good as they tasted. When Kiley had tried to put into words how light and nourishing Maya's food felt to her, Maya had nodded as if she understood fully and said, "That's because I put magic into it."

Kiley did not think she'd been joking.

Jack read from his phone. "Women's Clothing Line chiefly known for heavy duty outerwear, 1954 to 1982. It says here it was tough for women to find cold weather gear." Then he read, "'Women's coats were made to look nice. Men's were for actual protection against the elements. Women who worked outdoors had to buy men's coats, until JaVoe released its line of warm, attractive parkas made for women. Large, fur trimmed hoods were a JaVoe Coat trademark.'"

Kiley's bowl was empty. She felt sad and eyed how much was left in the pot. Enough that it wouldn't be rude to go for seconds?

"This was in the pocket." Chris held up his hand. A gold heart dangled from it by a delicate chain.

"Is that a locket?" Maya asked, leaving her own fabulous meal behind to hurry in there. "Can I see it, Chris?"

He snapped the chain, caught the charm, and pressed it into her hand. Maya fiddled with it until it popped open. And that launched the rest of them away from the meal that deserved so much better. They crowded together for a look. The locket had two photos, one in each side of the heart. In one, an older woman with a plump face, bronze skin, dark eyes that seemed weary and burdened. In the other, a young couple, arm in arm at an outdoor ice rink. They were obviously in love. She had dark hair like mink and was clearly not the same person as the older woman in the facing photo. The boy's hair was curly and brown. And they both had the saddest eyes she'd ever seen.

"Lay it on the table," Chris said. And when Maya did, he took a photo with his phone. "My notion is, we post these photos on social. 'Found this family heirloom. Looking for its rightful owner.' That sort of thing." He moved the phone closer, then back a little.

When he finished, he lifted his head, looking at the rest of them for consent. Maya shook her head. "It's gold. It's heavy, worth some money, maybe. How do we know some greedy liar won't come and claim it?"

"We ask them to show us a recognizable photo of the same people," Johnny replied. "If they're family, they'll have one."

"Makes sense to me," Kiley said. "Jack?"

He hadn't laid a hand on the locket yet. He still wasn't comfortable with his...abilities. He wasn't even sure what they were, except that he'd somehow been able to communicate with the murdered women in her basement. He'd seen their killer. He'd seen their deaths.

"I say post it," Jack said.

"Post it," Kiley repeated. Maya and Johnny nodded.

Chris tapped his phone. "Done."

"Good," Jack said. "Now enough work. This is supposed to be a celebration." He took Kiley by the arm and walked her back through to the dining room.

Johnny came with, but kept on going through to the kitchen, then returned with a bottle of wine in a bucket of ice. He poured for all, and then raised a glass, "Happy homecoming, Kiley."

Chris said, "Yeah, welcome back to spook central."

They all clinked glasses while Kiley tried not to get weirded out by his choice of words. That was exactly what she'd just said she did *not* want her house to become. She got a chill down her spine as she tipped up her glass for a long, long sip.

Jack caught her eye, and she knew he'd spend the night if she asked him to. But she wasn't going to ask him to. She had to see if she could do this. Sleep in her own house alone, like a grown up, now that the bodies of murder victims were no longer buried under her feet.

CHAPTER TWO

The Magic Shop

So, Jack thought, Kiley *really* didn't want to live with him.

Not that he wanted to rush into a full-on cohabitation thing. Hell, that was *way* down the line for them. He was in no hurry. What he couldn't figure out was why it bothered him so much that she wasn't either.

She'd stayed with him for six weeks and three days while her home had been a crime scene. He'd given her the guest room, but they'd spent most nights in his. And he thought it had gone pretty well. He thought she'd thought so, too. And yeah, she said it was because they were new, and living together put a lot of strain on a brand-new relationship, and that she'd just bought a house for fuck's sake—she said for fuck's sake a lot—all of which made perfect sense.

But his takeaway was still the same. She didn't want to live with him.

He probably should've emptied a closet for her. Maybe put

some plants around or something. If he wanted her to stay. Which he didn't. Duh.

"So what do you think?" Chris asked.

"Huh?" Jack looked up. He was standing in front of a shelf in his shop, staring at a display of tumbled gemstones and trying to remember why he'd come to this shelf to begin with.

Chris came up, took the carboard 15% off shelf-talker from his hand and slid it into its spot. "You okay, boss?"

"What? Yeah, yeah, sure I am. I was...thinking we need to order more amethyst."

"We ordered it yesterday." The kid's phone bleeped. He checked it, and said, "Here we go, here we go. It's on."

He only got that excited about ghost-related stuff. Chris was a real student of the woo-woo stuff. Probably knew more about the paranormal than those of them with... talents in that area. "What do you mean? What's on?"

"The people who responded to the locket post. They're two blocks away."

They'd got a hit on the photos within a couple hours of Chris posting them yesterday, but the owners couldn't come for it until tonight. Jack had told Chris to give them the shop address instead of, God forbid, Kylie's house. Even though it would be an awesome headquarters for their little gang of...whatever they were. It had the look and apparently, spooks liked it.

"We need a name," he said. He went to the front door and unlocked it, opened it up and stepped outside.

"For the group?" Chris came out behind him, zipped up his fleece-lined denim and flipped up the collar. "Ghostbusters is taken."

"And goofy. I want something serious."

"And creative, right? Like the name of your shop?!"

"What's wrong with The Magic Shop?"

"It states the obvious?"

Jack shrugged.

It was twenty after nine in late December and the village was deserted. No snow yet, but you could taste it on the air. All the shops up and down Main were lit up for the holidays and every sidewalk-facing window had a holiday scene in it. His own had a stack of new merch he was pushing, just lined in tinsel. The spirit boards were not moving at all, despite the stunning artwork in the collection he carried.

Chris had warned him people were funny about talking boards. The kid with the careless dreads and easy smile was a freaking genius. Not just about computers and social media, either. He was fascinated by everything paranormal, studied it like it was his job. Which it kind of was, working at a magic shop. More so now, given their new side gig helping clients with their ghost issues. Jack didn't want to even think about running the business without him.

A Mercedes veered off the road and into the strip in front of the shop. Jack flung his arm up too late to avoid being blinded by its headlights. When they shut off, he had to blink before he could see that they'd parked straddling two spaces. Car doors opened, closed. Shadow silhouettes got out, one from each side, and then they came toward him. A crispy downdraft chilled his nose. Yeah, snow was coming.

When they stepped into the pool of light that spilled from his front window onto the sidewalk, he got a look at them. A young couple who looked enough alike to be related. Same dark hair and brows, same oval faces, and something about their brown eyes.

"Jack McCain?" The woman said, extending a slender, manicured hand. "Sara Cantrell." She shook with a grip that felt stronger than her hand looked. "And this is my brother, Kev."

Kev just nodded, not moving to shake.

"Brother and sister," Chris said. "Twins?" He opened the door and held it for them.

"Yeah." Kev muttered as they walked inside. They stopped near the counter, looking around the place.

"So you're some kind of new ager?" Sara asked.

"It's that kind of town. Please, follow me." Jack led, and Chris brought up the rear.

Kiley was running late, and that worried him a little, which was stupid, but he couldn't help it. Last time she'd lived in that place, she'd been in real danger. He thought it was nuts that she'd wanted to spend her first night back alone. But he got it. She had something to prove, probably only to herself. Maybe to any ghosts who might be paying attention.

They went through the curtains at the back of the shop into the private room where he offered readings and guidance. It was cozy back there, comfortable. Round table with padded chairs all around it, red tablecloth. People expected a red tablecloth. He'd never quite figured out why. There were chimes positioned right in front of the air vents, so they tinkled very gently whenever the heat or AC came on. The lights were in the corners, and recessed, rather than directly over the table, and there was a dimmer switch. Ambience was half the deal in this line of work.

Sara crossed her arms and said, "Tell me you're not about to suggest a seance, Mr. McCain."

"I was going to suggest refreshments. Coffee, tea, cocoa?"

"Whiskey?" Kev asked.

"No, not in the shop, sorry."

"Let's just get on with this," his sister said. "I want to see the locket."

"Sure." He nodded at Chris to watch them, because something about them made him uneasy. Maybe it was just that *they* were uneasy. Nervous. He didn't get the feeling they were unfriendly people as a rule. But they were not happy to be there. Maybe it was the subject.

He returned to the front of the shop, went behind the register and popped open the drawer. Just as he lifted the locket out, the shop door jangled. He knew it was Kiley before he even looked up. He felt her, always. Used to make the hair on the back of his neck stand up. Now it made other parts react the same way. "Late, much?" He asked, because the alternative was to pull her into his arms as if he hadn't seen her in a week instead of just a day.

She came in, around the counter, stood on tiptoe and kissed his chin. "I missed you, too."

"Missed me? We just saw each other yesterday. Get a grip."

"Okay." She grabbed the front of his jeans, gave a squeeze, laughed softly. She was clearly trying to kill him. "They here, yet?"

"In the back."

She held up her phone. "If that's their car, I snapped the plates. Just in case. Come on." She headed back without waiting for him. He lowered his head to hide his smile in case she turned around, then he watched her walk because, hello, male. Then he followed her.

"My associate, Kiley Brigham," he said when he came through the curtains behind her. "Kiley these are the Cantrells, Sara and Kevin."

"Kev," Sara corrected sharply.

"Kev," Jack said. "Sorry. You must get that all the time."

"It's fine."

"They're twins," Chris said, like it was important information Kiley ought to know.

Jack opened the locket and laid it, face-up, on the table. "Is this your grandmother?"

"May I?" Kev asked before reaching for it. Jack nodded and he picked it up, brought it closer. "Yes, yes, that's Grandma Nisha." He handed the locket to his sister. "And that's Mom," she said, her thumb touching the face of the beautiful teenage girl in the other photo. "With our father."

"Did you bring—" Kiley began.

Before she could finish the question, Sara pulled an old-fashioned photo album from her oversized bag, set it on the table and slid it across. Kiley pulled out a chair and sat down. "She's even wearing this very locket in some of these," she said. "And we have a couple of others taken that day at the ice rink, Grandma Nisha isn't in many, since she was the one taking them. They're mostly shots of our mom and dad, some of the only photos of our parents together. But I don't remember this one ever being in Grandma's locket before." Then she looked across the table at Jack and said, "Where did you say you found this?"

Jack looked at Kiley. They'd discussed this. What to say. How much to reveal. No ghost stuff. It was too soon.

"It was in the pocket of a coat I found on my front porch yesterday," Kiley said, just like they'd planned. She glanced down at the photo album as she turned its pages. She saw other photos taken at the same place and time as the one of the younger couple in Grandma Nisha's locket, the twins' parents as teens. Always together. Never smiling. They seemed haunted or heartbroken. She turned a page, then tilted her head to one side, and pressed her finger to a snapshot. "That's the same coat."

She pushed the album back across to Sara so she could see while Jack tried to tell her to rein it in and not cross the line into spook territory.

"Grandma Nisha loved that coat." Sara frowned at them. "So, you're telling me that some stranger randomly left a coat just like my dead grandmother's coat, and her locket with my parents' photo in it, at *your* front door?"

Kiley leaned forward. "That's what I'm telling you, yeah."

"Dude, I was there when it happened," Chris said. "Doorbell rang, nothing but a coat. I'm not saying it's not crazy AF, but it happened."

"And we'd like to figure out why," Jack said. He was using a tone he'd used in the past, back when he used to call his clients his patients. "Do you mind telling me about your grandmother? Grandma Nisha?"

"Her maiden name was Patel," Kev said, just when Sara opened her mouth to say no way in hell. "Third generation Indian-American. Married an Irishman, Edward O'Reilly Cantrell. Used to joke about going from Patel to Cantrell. We never met Edward. He died before we were born."

Kiley shifted back in her seat, settling in as if to hear a story. "What was she like, your grandma Nisha?"

Kev looked at his sister. She pressed her lips, lowered her chin, closed her eyes in silent consent.

He returned the slightest nod. "It was cancer," he said.

"It was heartbreak." Sara was staring straight ahead, visibly refusing to allow a single emotion to escape. "Our mother, Rosalie," she put her finger on the teenage ice skater in the photo album as she said the name, "is Grandma Nisha's only daughter. She attempted suicide five years ago and she's been in a persistent vegetative state ever since. Grandma Nisha never got over that."

"Rosalie," Jack said. Something was itching at his memory.

He could tell Kiley wanted to ask more, but he caught her eye and gave a subtle head shake. She picked up the message. He opened the album, looked for a photo of their mother later in life, like maybe five years ago, before her suicide attempt. "Rosalie Cantrell." And then he found one, he sank into an empty chair without thinking about it. It was like his bones had gone liquid. Rosalie Cantrell stared up at him from a photograph.

He looked at Sara, and saw Grandma Nisha standing right behind her, wearing her big red parka, her face hidden deep within the cavernous fur-trimmed hood.

"What?" He asked her. And then Kiley was out of her chair and standing behind him with her hands on his shoulders. "It's not ringing any bells," she said. "So your mother…is she still…?"

Sara sat back, said nothing. Kev nodded, and said, "Yes, she's still alive, still in a coma. What do you think this means?"

"Oh, come on, Kev, it's some kind of scam," Sara said, like she was reporting the weather. "Our dead grandma has a message for us about our comatose mother from beyond the grave. This guy can tell us what it is for a modest fee."

"It's only a scam if I'm selling something," Jack said. "And I'm not. I don't know what it means. I do know that Kiley's house, where your grandmother showed up, has had a lot of...activity."

"Ghosts, it's had ghosts," Kiley blurted. She pushed her lower lip out to blow her hair off her forehead. He loved when she did that.

Sara Cantrell rose from her seat. "We don't believe in ghosts. That kind of bullshit is dangerous."

"Tell me about it!" Kiley got up, too. "Look, lady, I opened my door, and somebody was standing there wearing that coat. And then she collapsed, and when we picked her up, there was only the coat with nobody in it. I don't know why the dead would show up on my doorstep, but I know a ghost when I see one cause it's not my first trip around that particular carrot patch."

"Carrot patch?"

"You think I'm enjoying this shit? I'm not. I just want to be left the hell alone to settle into my new house and enjoy the holidays. Okay? That's all I want." She threw her hands up, waved them down in a fuck you all gesture, and turned to pace away. She only went as far as the curtain, but Jack thought it wouldn't take much to push her through it.

"A lot of people died in her house," Chris said quietly. He was sitting, and his voice was soft. "So that's a lot of traffic moving from this side to the other side. Maybe it created a kind of highway. A path." Everyone had turned to stare at him. Chris dipped his head to hide an embarrassed grin. "It's a theory in progress."

There was a lull of silence, and then Jack asked, "What did you mean, Sara, when you said 'this stuff is dangerous?'"

"You don't think it's dangerous?"

"Sure I do. In my case, it's based on experience. But why do *you* think it's dangerous?"

She shot a look at her brother. Jack could've sworn they had a verbal exchange with nothing but their eyes. Freaking twins were creepy.

Sara looked at him with eerie timing. "Ghost stories can destroy a fragile mind. They can ruin lives. They can tear apart families. And you should be ashamed of yourself for being a part of that." She picked up the locket. "I want the coat and I want to get out of here. This conversation is making me very uncomfortable."

Chris got up and went to the closet, opened it, and pulled the coat down. Jack had zipped it into a plastic blanket holder. Maya and Johnny had gone over the thing first. They'd taken photos, a fabric sample, checked the lining, meditated with it, the whole nine. And they had close-up shots of the locket and the photos it held. He hoped they wouldn't regret giving up the evidence.

When Chris closed the closet door, Grandma Nisha was standing behind it and Jack gasped aloud, then tried to cover it by coughing into his fist. But the whole time he looked over his knuckles at the ghost of Grandma Nisha. Or at least, her coat. Her face was still hidden somewhere in the cave-hood. Her legs faded out at mid-calf, where he thought he could just detect the furry tops of her winter boots.

Jack hated this. He'd been perfectly content pretending to be a psychic while giving people psychologically sound advice. Finding out he really had some kind of connection to the dead had turned his world upside down.

Working with the victims buried in Kiley's basement had opened a door. If her house *was* some sort of ghost super highway, then he was the service area where every traveler stopped for snacks and coffee.

To be honest, the whole seeing dead people thing gave him the creeps.

Sara scooped the locket off the table. "Come on, Kev. Bring the coat." Then she was heading out through the shop, past Kiley and through the curtains without even acknowledging her presence.

Kev gathered up the coat and followed, never making eye contact with anyone on the way.

The bell jangled as they exited the shop.

They all stood there staring at each other for a long moment. And then Chris read the room and said, "I'll lock up the front door on my way out. You guys can get the back?"

"Yeah," Jack said. "We'll get the gang together tomorrow to talk about this."

"Okay, yeah. What do you think, lunch hour?"

"Yeah."

"You good with that Kiley?" Chris asked.

"Yeah, sure, noon is fine."

"Cool. Hey, I'll tell everybody. We'll all bring food, don't worry about it, Kiley." Chris left, bells jingled, locks turned.

Kiley lowered her head and muttered, "Oh, God, he assumed we'd meet at my house."

Jack felt her looking at him, awaiting a response, but he was still looking at the ghost.

"We didn't get a chance to ask them any details about their Grandma Nisha's death."

Jack sat down. He tapped a button under the table and the drawer slid open. Inside, there was a brass flask with some really smooth whiskey in it, and a pair of monogrammed shot glasses. A gift from a client.

He set them up and poured. "They found her lying under the apple tree in her back yard. I think she planned to be buried there, with her husband and daughter. It popped in. Just that little piece of it, with her sitting on the ground against the tree trunk, facing her daughter Rosalie's bedroom window."

"Is she here, right now?" Kiley asked, reading him almost as well as he read dead people.

He nodded. "You don't see her this time?"

"No."

"Damn." He looked at the floor.

Kiley reached over and put a hand on his cheek. "Stay with me tonight?"

"At the haunted mansion?"

She nodded hard. It meant something to her, reclaiming her space from the dead. Like she had to show them who was boss.

He lifted his head and Grandma Nisha was gone. He said, "Let's grab a few things out of the shop on the way, huh?" He downed his drink, went back into the main part of the store and took a book off the shelf. She downed hers and followed.

"What kinds of things?" she asked.

He held up the book. "Essential Magic. It's by Maya, our Maya, and it has a chapter on setting wards around your home to keep out anything you don't want in. Human or otherwise. I skimmed it earlier." He handed her the book, then took a cloth shopping bag bearing the shop's triple moon logo from behind the counter, and returned to the shelves. He took a couple jars of herbs, a bottle of holy water, a packet of black salt, and several stones and dropped them into the bag.

"Oh, it's gonna be like that, is it?" she asked, her tone teasing, maybe to counteract his sudden tension. "You're gonna go all Dr. Peter Venkman on me, now? Impress me by solving my little ghost problem?"

"Worked the last time." He smiled and realized he'd probably been a lot more fun before he'd started seeing dead people.

She turned her phone toward him. It showed a color photo of the pizza she'd just ordered. "You gather your kinds of supplies. I'll gather mine."

"You're a mind-reader, Brigham. You just don't know it."

"Screw ghosts. I read takeout orders." She dropped her voice to a whisper. "Before you even know you want to order them." And then she made spooky fingers and went "Ooo-eee-ooo-ooo."

He smiled and his heart hurt. "So, I never told you that um… before I came here and opened this shop, I um…was a psychiatrist."

Her smile froze and faded at about the same pace she lowered her phone-holding hand. "You were what now?"

"A shrink. And Rosalie Cantrell was the reason I quit."

CHAPTER THREE

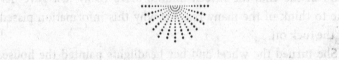

"Rosalie Cantrell, the teenage girl in the skating photos, daughter of Grandma Nisha the parka-wearing ghost, was one of my patients," Jack said.

Kiley looked around the shop. "Is this really where we want to have this conversation? Cause I'm thinking I might want to drink more, and I'd prefer not to have to drive after."

"Not that you would," he said.

"Never," she said, hand to heart. "So you get in your shop van and I'll get in my car, and we'll have this discussion at my place in fifteen minutes. Okay?"

He nodded. "Okay."

"Okay." She thrust her hand into her pocket and jiggled her keys for luck, then headed for the back door, pushed it open, paused and looked back. "You didn't fuck her, did you?"

"No! God, no, what the—"

"Just checking." And she went out.

The fifteen-minute drive would, Kiley thought, give her time to digest what he had just told her. He used to be a psychiatrist. Which wasn't a bad sort of secret, but it just begged the question, what the hell else didn't she know about him? Why he would keep something like that from her?

Man, she'd known he wasn't ready for anything serious with her, but to not even tell her the most basic stuff? Like that he had a Ph.D., for example.

Jesus.

So in the end, the fifteen-minute drive really just gave her time to think of the many reasons why this information pissed her the fuck off.

She turned the wheel and her headlights painted the house. No disembodied spirits were peeking out the windows at her, and no empty coats were bundled on the porch. Thank goodness.

The trees had gone bare. It would snow soon. Her house was going to look stunning in the snow.

She really needed to decorate.

Jack's headlights shut off as soon as they were pointing her way, because he was just that considerate. The ass. Why hadn't he told her?

He got out, closed the door, thrust his hands into his jeans' front pockets. She got out, too. He looked like a kid who'd tracked dirt on his mom's carpet, sorry and too adorable to be mad at.

She turned away, because she needed to be pissed for a little bit longer. As she unlocked the big front door and went inside and hit the passcode, she said, "Why didn't you tell me?"

"It's not you. I don't tell anyone. Because I'm ashamed, I suppose."

His voice broke a little. She turned around, took his hands, and pulled him into the living room, to the sofa. She set him down, and went to pour drinks from the decanter that was still out from its last use, then handed him a glass and sat down.

They were angled, facing each other, on the sofa. He said, "It's my fault, what happened to poor Rosalie Cantrell. She um...she told me she could see the ghost of her first love, a boy she said died when she was only fifteen. He'd been haunting her ever since her sixteenth birthday, she said. She was forty, forty-one when she came to me. Came to me looking for someone to believe her, instead of trying to medicate her ghosts away."

Kiley nodded slow. "What reasonable shrink would believe a patient could see the dead?"

"One who could see them, too."

"But you couldn't then. Or wouldn't or didn't know you could, or something." She rose up off the sofa and paced to the fireplace, wishing there was a fire to go with it. "Do you think that's why Rosalie's mother came here? That she was trying to come to you for help?"

"Help with what?"

"Crossing over, for one thing. I mean, if she were at peace, she wouldn't be playing peek-a-boo with a haunted parka, would she?"

He stiffened and nodded. "That makes sense. She wants something from me."

"There you go."

"She wants the same thing she wanted from me five years ago. She wanted me to help her daughter. And I failed."

The doorbell rang and broke the unbearable tension of trying to figure out what to say. "It's okay" seemed kind of unequal to the moment. She settled for, "Pizza's here."

"I'll get it." Jack got up and went to the door.

Kiley went to the kitchen, and not because she wanted to eat her pizza from a plate. She needed a minute.

She'd planned to ask Jack to stay tonight anyway. Last night, on her own, she'd been fine until she tried to sleep. And then she kept getting trapped in nightmares where those poor dead women floated up through her floorboards and through her bed and through her body. They'd clutched her from the outside and somehow from within as well, to drag her down with them, back to that concrete prison cell underneath her basement.

She knew they were not real. The dead women had been exhumed, identified, and re-buried. They'd had funerals with family all around, with flowers and markers and tears, the way it should have been all along. They were at peace.

Her nightmares had little to do with those women, and everything to do with her own fears and insecurities. She'd wanted to call Jack a dozen times last night. And then when she'd seen him so shaken up at the shop, she'd jumped on a second, less selfish reason. And now she was more concerned about his well-being than her own.

This was a lot. This was huge. And he'd only known he had his abilities for a few weeks and he was far from coming to terms with them. He didn't like seeing ghosts. She knew that. She didn't much care for it, either. But there was more going on with him. This time, it was personal.

They sat on the sofa watching TV and pigging out on junk food, and it was good. They'd decided to sleep on this whole thing tonight and decide their next move tomorrow.

"Grandma Nisha's grandkids are dicks, aren't they?" Kiley asked during a commercial break.

"I don't think so. Sara's angry, yeah so maybe a bit of a dick. Kev seemed...broken."

A frown knitted her brow. "What do you mean?"

"I don't know. Didn't you think he seemed kind of..."

"Sad?"

"Pain-wracked."

"So, *really* sad?" Kiley dropped her crust into the open pizza box. "But what I want to talk about is you. Are you okay?"

He put his pizza back into the box. "At the moment, yeah. I'm just...frequently re-evaluating."

She pursed her lips and nodded. "Well, listen, I'm just gonna say it. I know we're new, and not in a hurry, but... I'm here for you. I'm on your side, you know? I'm your...you know."

He looked at her face for a long moment, and then he nodded, and said, "Thank you." And then, "Me, too. For you, I mean."

He leaned in and kissed her, then they leaned against each other, and reached for second slices.

"Grandma Nisha wasn't happy we let the granddaughter take the locket, I can tell you that much," Jack said at length.

Kiley bit in, thinking and chewing. After a swallow she said, "I wonder why I couldn't see her at the shop, but I could see her on my porch."

"I think she wanted you to see her on the porch."

"They can control who can see them?"

"I don't know. Maybe."

"But why would she want me to see her?"

"I don't know. I just don't know."

The doorbell jangled and she dropped her slice right into her lap. Jack laughed softly. "Jumpy much?"

"I'm not jumpy. You're jumpy." She returned her all but unused plate to the coffee table and grabbed a napkin to clean the cheese and sauce triangle outline from her jeans.

Jack got up and went to the door. He opened it without saying "Who is it?" Or anything like that. Kiley rose, turning while still swiping the napkin over her denim. And then she just went still. Because he'd opened the door and that damn coat was standing there again. No legs holding it up, and no face hiding in the depths of the hood.

"Um, hey Brigham?"

"I see it."

Jack cleared his throat and Kiley forced her feet to move up beside him, because nobody should stand face-to-empty hood with a ghost all alone. She slid her arm through his to let him know she was there and he finally managed to say, "What do you want?"

27

A shrieking face emerged from that hood. Its mouth was wide, eyes bulging, and its wail should've blown their hair back. They staggered backwards, arm in arm, and Kiley covered her ears and buried her face in Jack's chest. He wrapped his arms around her, cringing away from the screamer. And then the sound died so completely that Kiley heard the coat drop to the porch floor, just like it had done before.

Jack lifted his head first. "It's okay. It's… gone. Sort of." He was still holding her close, but she turned to look and whispered every cuss word she knew. He tried to remove his arms from around her, but she clutched them and held them where they were. So then he crept forward, and she sort of crept too, because she was clinging so tight it seemed she was trying to climb inside his clothes, and not for fun and sexy reasons.

He stretched out one arm and picked up the coat, bringing it inside with them. Kiley shoved the door closed, only then easing out of the circle of his arms.

He was holding the coat by the shoulders, letting it dangle. "Check the pockets."

"*You* check the pockets," he shot back. Then, "I-I'm holding the coat."

She shook her head, but stiffened her spine and shoved her hand into the right pocket. There was something in the bottom. She brought it out and let it dangle from its chain. "There's zero chance Grandma Nisha's grand-shits don't accuse us of stealing this."

"Why would we return it to them just to steal it back?" Jack took the locket, pried it open, looked at the photos inside.

Kiley took the coat from him while he did, and checked it inside and out, six ways to Sunday, label and all, but found nothing. It was brand new. Still had a price tag dangling from the end of one sleeve. She took hold of that, turned it slowly. $7.50 was stamped on one side. "Milner's Department Store" on the other.

With a curious frown, she grabbed her cell phone off the table and took a shot of each side. Then she went online and started searching.

"Milner's Department Store had five locations in New York State at its peak in, 1975. It was bought out and closed down by a chain...." *Tap, tap, tap.* "A chain that is no longer in business, either.

She looked up, because Jack was looking at the photo through a magnifying glass. "Look, look at this," he said.

Kiley bent her head to gaze at the locket through the glass, not at Grandma Nisha but at the young couple, Rosalie and her beau.

"There's something...." And then suddenly, he jerked his head back and dropped the locket onto the coffee table. "Jesus, did you see that?"

She picked up the locket, took the magnifying glass from him, and peered through it, but she didn't see anything.

"What did you see?"

"The guy. He blinked, and then looked me right in the eye."

"Rosalie's boyfriend?" She met his eyes. He looked pretty shaken up. She supposed she would be too if a photo came to life on her. "You think we should call the Cantrell twins and tell them their grandma's coat and locket ran away from home again?"

"In the morning," he said. He sank onto the sofa and let his head fall back against its cushion. "I need to shut my brain down for a while."

"Might I suggest a hot shower?"

He picked up his head. "If it's for two, you might."

She smiled, warmed right to her toes by the look in his eyes. She took his hands He got up, pulled her in close for a long, slow, sexy kiss. Kiley couldn't think of too many things that felt better than his lips on hers. So soft, so tasty.

Damn. She'd missed him last night. What the hell was she supposed to make of that?

He nibbled her lower lip, and her brain shut down. Thank goodness.

~

Kiley kept her eyes on Jack across the breakfast table. It had been a good night. Just really…good. They were kind of like clockwork in bed.

There had been, she thought, an interesting shift in dynamic. Before, she'd been scared shitless and he'd been…well, scared shitless, too, but also, her support. Now, she sensed he might be the one who was going to need support. He'd needed her last night, she was sure of that much. The sex had felt like a healing.

He'd slept like a log until the wee hours. Then he'd tossed around and muttered in his sleep. He'd never done that before. He wasn't himself.

The twist-and-ring doorbell chirruped.

"I swear to God, if it's that fucking coat again–" Kiley got up. "Stay, hon. Eat your breakfast." French Toast. They'd made it together, sort of. Really he'd done all the work. Said it was his specialty. Sappiest shit ever, she knew. "I've got this."

"It won't be her," Jack said. "Nisha likes to show up on dark and stormy nights, not bright, sunny mornings."

Kiley went to the door. Jack, ignoring her instructions, followed. Before they got there, the bell was twisted a second time, and pounding on the door followed.

"I'm coming. Don't have a stroke." She said it loud enough to be sure they heard, already guessing who "they" were.

She wasn't disappointed. A raging beast and her nutless brother stood at the door. Twins, huh? Apparently the female got all the balls.

Kev's head was down. Sara was looking Kiley right in the eye. "My grandmother's coat was stolen last night and–oh my God. Oh. My. God, it's right there!"

Kiley opened the door wider and waved them through. "We were going to call you after breakfast, having decided that both–

ering people any earlier on a weekend morning would be indecent."

Missing the sarcasm entirely, Sara strode into the house and picked up the coat.

"Locket's in the pocket," Kiley told her, wishing she'd thought of a non-rhyming way to convey the info.

"Don't be ridiculous. I'm *wearing* the locket." Sara pressed a hand to her smooth, twenty-five-year-old décolleté as she spoke, then her eyebrows bent into the kind of angry frown kids draw on monsters with black crayons. "What the hell is going on here?" She grabbed up the coat and checked its pockets almost violently.

"Your coat showed up on my porch last night, same way it did before. Doorbell rang, I opened the door. The coat was standing there as if occupied, then fell to the floor as if vacant with the locket in the… with the necklace in the pocket."

"Bullshit." Sara had found the locket, held it dangling from her hand.

"Well, what do you think happened, Sara? You think we broke into your home last night, stole the coat, took the necklace off you while you slept, hypnotized you not to notice when you got up this morning, and brought it back here just to throw it on our sofa and give it back to you all over again?"

"The coat wasn't at her house. It was at mine," Kev said. He kept his voice low, but at least picked up his head when he spoke. He had dark brown eyes, close cropped dark brown hair, and possibly, Kiley admitted reluctantly, a soul. "I'm sure nobody came into Grandma's house last night. The alarm was set. And I barely slept."

"You didn't tell me that." His sister's frown eased into what looked like concern as she replaced the locket around her neck.

"It was a bad night," he replied.

"So you live at your grandma Nisha's house?" Jack asked.

"We've always lived there," Kev said. All of us, until Sara moved out. Mom was never...she was never well."

"I know." Jack lowered his head when he said it. "Listen, I need to tell you something. I used to practice psychiatry. Your mother, Rosalie, was my patient for a short time."

Kiley watched the twins' reactions. Kev looked from Jack, to his sister, to the open front door as if unsure what to do. After a panicked second, he closed the door, but he didn't come further inside.

"How did your mother...hurt herself?" Kiley asked.

"Injected herself with Grandma Nisha's insulin." Sara spoke slowly and Kiley heard a hint of accusation in her voice for the first time. "But it wasn't enough, or maybe Gram found her too soon. So she didn't die. She's just ... there. There's no feeding tube, because she can take food by mouth. But there's nobody in there. There hasn't been for a long time."

"You must have been just kids," Kiley said.

Sara nodded. "She missed our twentieth birthday by a month."

"I'm so sorry," Jack said. Kiley could hear the tremor in his voice. He wasn't only sorry, he was guilty. "I am so horribly sorry."

They looked at him, both of them. Kev nodded once, as if to say "It's okay." But Sara just kept staring and whispered, "Our grandmother called you Quack McCain. She hated you. She said it was all your fault. You were the last shrink our mother saw before she did it."

He nodded. "Yeah, it probably was my fault," he said very slowly. And then, he lifted his head, looked them in the eyes, and said, "I think I need to see her."

Sara moved as if to get to her feet, but her quiet brother put a hand on her shoulder and got up himself instead. He looked at Jack, right into his eyes. "You're the guy who ruined our lives, man. You took our mother."

"He's the guy who tried to *help* your mother." Kiley inserted herself between them on the word "help," her arms awkwardly out from her sides. The men backed away from each other.

"Tell them, Jack," she said. "It's their mother, come on. Tell them all of it. They have a right to know."

"They're not gonna believe–"

"Tell them."

Jack took a deep breath, then another. "Your mother insisted she was being haunted by a dead person. And I didn't believe her."

"*Wow*. What a newsflash. Like we didn't grow up with *that* bullshit our entire lives," Sara said. "She told everyone that. She was claiming to see the ghost of our dead father before we were even born. *Nobody* believed her."

"Well, maybe we should have." It was hard for Jack to say, Kiley knew it. She was proud of him for saying it anyway.

"We should have believed she could see a ghost?" Sara asked. "Mr. McCain, there are no such things as ghosts."

The doorbell rang.

"I saw one in that photo, in the locket," Jack said.

Sara put her hand up to her chest to touch the locket again, but it was not there.

The doorbell rang again.

"Let's answer the door, everybody," Kiley said. She took Sara by the hand like they were besties and tugged. Jack came right behind, one hand on Kev's shoulder.

Kiley reached out and opened the door.

The coat stood there all by itself. Everybody screamed, and somebody slammed the door in its face. "Ten to one, your locket's in its pocket," Kiley said to Sara, and she didn't give a shit about the cutesy rhyme anymore.

Kev uncurled himself from his one-legged upright fetal pose, smoothed the front of his shirt, and said, "When did you say you want to see our mother?"

CHAPTER FOUR

hey pulled into the driveway of a great big Victorian house in pristine condition. It was bright white with black trim, on a street where it and several other houses of the same style stood like queens among the commoners—the smaller, modern cracker boxes that had sprung up around them. But the Victorians were the grande dames. Their daffodils had been blooming for a hundred years. They were the neighborhood matriarchs and most of their fancy trim work was painted in currently trendy pastels. But not Grandma Nisha Cantrell's house. Black and white, and more dignified for it. And yet there was a sadness about the place. While her neighbors were cheery and playful with their colors, she stood alone, stark and solemn, dressed for a funeral.

Up close, the white paint was starting to peel in a few places. There was a painted wrought iron fence around the dooryard, but rust showed through here and there, where small flakes of white paint had chipped off.

Jack looked at Kiley, glad he was with her. They'd had a good night. Okay, they'd had a great night. And then a long, fattening breakfast together. He was trying not to analyze it and just let it have been what it was. It didn't mean that anything had changed.

"So you didn't see ghosts...back then?" Kiley asked.

They'd been talking again on the drive over to the Cantrell house. He didn't used to like talking about himself, his history, his inner life. But with her it was never hard or weird.

"I never saw ghosts until those ones at your place. I just...gave good advice. I felt like if I pretended to believe and played along and doled out psychologically sound therapy, I could help people."

"The way you tried to help Rosalie."

"Yeah. I remember thinking back then that she'd have believed some crackpot psychic more easily than she would believe me, her doctor. And then she did what she did, and...."

"And you've blamed yourself ever since. Even became a crackpot psychic yourself."

"I thought all this time that my mistake was not playing along. That I should've pretended to believe her and worked around it." He shook his head, staring up at the imposing house. "It never even occurred to me her claims were real."

"It wouldn't have occurred to anybody, Jack." Kiley touched his hand.

All by itself, his hand flipped around and clasped hers. It was automatic. He used to think he couldn't stand Kiley Brigham. It was starting to feel like that had always been a lie. A way to deny what was going on in his heart.

He met her eyes and smiled. "You're trying to pep-talk me straight through this thing, aren't you, Brigham?"

"Giving it a shot. It's not my specialty. Am I doing it right?"

"Just right."

She rolled her eyes like he was being ridiculous while smiling her face off.

They got out of the car. Dark clouds skittered over the sun

and the wind picked up. The air still tasted like snow, but none had manifested yet.

Kiley moved closer, which was hard since they were already touching. He let go of her hand to slide his arm around her shoulders and they slow-walked their way up the sidewalk. Dry, dead leaves skittered across in front of them. The steps were wooden, white with gray risers. The wrought iron railing was newer than the fence on the lawn, which had to be original. The front porch was full-width with white wicker furniture and a swing.

"They could at least sweep off the leaves," Jack said for no reason at all.

Kiley sent him a WTF look.

He shrugged. "Sorry. I don't think that was me." He knocked on the door.

Kev opened it. Sara stood behind him, rubbing her arms and looking uncomfortable. "Well, come in, it's freezing out," she said. "Let's get this over with. I hate this place."

She didn't used to hate it, though. Jack got a brief glimpse of a pigtailed little girl sliding down the bannister and squealing. He almost smiled, but realized it wouldn't have been appropriate to the situation. Kev was somber and nervous. Sara was uncomfortable and hostile. And Kiley was...she was watching him closer than a tightrope walker's spotter.

It felt good to know she had his back.

Inside, he half expected to see Rosalie as he remembered her. A forty-something single mother of two nineteen-year-olds, with all the normal stresses and worries that brought, complicated by uncontrolled mental illness and a very real ghost.

He'd lumped those two things together. That had been a mistake.

The house looked like you'd expect the Victorian home of a grandmother to look, heavy on the jewel tones, allpaper with roses, knick-knacks everywhere. Photos of people and pets cluttered every surface in stand up frames. It smelled like moth balls and Ben Gay.

"Let's get this over with," Sara said. "She's upstairs. Come on."

Jack followed and wondered why he felt so uneasy. He tried to pay attention to his feelings as Chris was always telling him to do. His heart was going too fast. He could feel it fluttering now and then, like it was skipping beats. He followed Sara up the stairs with Kiley right behind him and Kev behind her. She led them to a corner bedroom, all the way at the end of the hall.

Sara opened the door and walked in, about halfway to the bed, then turned to waved her arm at him to come in, already.

Jack had come to a stop in the doorway because of the guy who stood at the foot of Rosalie Cantrell's the hospital bed. He'd turned toward them when they'd walked in. He had a mass of tangled dark hair, and his face was smeared in streaks of black and red paint, to the point where you couldn't tell his skin tone. He wore an olive drab jacket, unbuttoned over emptiness, and he faded to nothing about knee level.

Jack glimpsed him then quickly looked away, careful not to meet his eyes. Something in his gut told him not to let on that he could see this one. Not this one. This one was angry.

Kiley's hand closed on his forearm. Kev walked right through the guy and bent over the bed. "Hey, Mom, I brought a visitor."

Jack walked around the ghost. He couldn't bring himself to walk through it, but he couldn't see Rosalie past its putrid presence. It stank. Why did it stink?

Rosalie lay on her back, eyes open and moving in a repetitive pattern, upper left, lower right, upper left, lower right. She wasn't seeing anything. He could barely sense any level of consciousness in her. He could usually feel a kind of energetic hum from other people. It was getting louder, and he was reading up on how to tune it out at will. Hasn't figured it out yet.

There was no energy buzz in Rosalie. This was a body acting mainly on impulse's from a barely functioning brain. Consciousness had receded like a wave hissing away from the shore. But she still existed. Her soul still existed, and maybe he could reach that part of her.

He said, "Hello, Rosalie. It's Doctor McCain. I don't know if you remember me, but–"

The eye movements stopped. So did the very slight bobbing of her head that had accompanied them. She went still.

"I've come to apologize. I'm sorry I didn't believe you before, when you told me about your ghost. I know better now. I thought I should tell you that."

She was silent and unmoving.

He leaned closer and said it again, "I'm very sorry I didn't believe you, Rosalie."

She roared like an angry bear, swung her arms and kicked her legs. Her IV pole crashed over onto his head and her entire body thrashed in the bed.

Kev grabbed hold of his mother from the other side of the bed, while Kiley helped Jack get up and untangled from the IV lines while. Rosalie pushed her son off like a WWE wrestler, and he went stumbling backward and smashed into the dresser, knocking a box to the floor. Jewelry and other small items flew everywhere.

Rosalie went still again. She lay staring straight into the eyes of the ghost at the foot of the bed. He said something, frustrated that she couldn't hear. That no one could. And then she closed hers and seemed to sleep.

The ghost turned his way too quickly. He caught Jack looking back at him before Jack averted his eyes. Too late, he felt it.

He straightened the I.V. pole, moving it back to its former position. Kev picked himself up off the floor, looking around at the spilled items at his feet. The jewelry box was broken, its lid snapped off at one hinge.

Sara said, "Guess it's safe to say she remembers you."

"Guess so," Jack said. The ghost was coming over to him, so he walked to the other side of the bed as if to see what Kev was up to. "Sorry about the box."

"Isn't that the one that was locked?" Sara asked.

Kev nodded. "We've never had the key. She gets agitated if we touch it, so we don't."

"But this time, she got agitated *until* you touched it," Kiley said. "I wonder if that means anything."

Jack looked at the items on the floor. He saw quite a lot of jewelry, a set of keys, a small book that looked like some kind of a diary, a fancy perfume bottle, a lock of hair in a ribbon, a–

Her diary!

He didn't hear it so much as feel the dead guy's words, and obediently, his eyes shifted back to the small book. It was leather-bound, with a tiny hasp and padlock that was still locked. The lid had detached from the hinged side.

"We're done here," Sara said. "This can't have been good for her, getting so agitated like that. Please get out."

Jack looked at Kiley. Then he shifted his eyes to the little book on the floor, and without missing a beat she said, "Oh my gosh, what is that?" and she pointed. When Sara and Kev looked where she was pointing, she picked up the book and an earring, pock-eted the book, and held the earring out in an open palm smoother than butter. "I guess it was just a shadow. All this ghost stuff gets to me. Here, Kev, you almost missed this."

Smooth.

Kev took the earring and said, "Thanks," while Sara clearly sensed something off.

The ghost glared too, right at Jack, just about daring him to look back. And then he realized he didn't need to look back. The spook, whoever he was, felt Jack's awareness of him. It wasn't about physical eyes looking at physical things.

Jack was pretty sure nobody else could see the guy. Except for Rosalie, somehow. It occurred to Jack that maybe he wasn't seeing with his eyes when he saw spirits. And this angry one with the painted face knew Jack could see him. He had a feeling this wasn't the last he'd see of the guy.

"We'll go. But before we do, what was your father's name?" Jack asked. "You never said."

"None of your business. No more snooping around in our family's painful past. Just. Get. Out."

~

"So?" Kiley asked. She got behind the wheel of her beloved Leaping Lana, rust brown and ancient, but reliable, and twisted the key. Lana belched to life obediently. The car was a tank. The local mechanic said he could keep her running for as long as he could keep finding spare parts, but that what she really needed was a whole new body, which Kiley thought was a rude thing to say right in front of Lana.

She backed into the street, shifted into drive, and pulled the book out of her blouse simultaneously. "I'm not sure how I feel about taking this, but…" She handed it to Jack. "What did she communicate with you from her coma?"

"No. She's not floating around outside her body. She's in there. Just way down deep. Mostly unconscious."

"Do you think she's… trapped?"

"I don't know. If she is, I imagine it has something to do with the dead guy hanging out by her bedside."

"There was a dead guy by her bedside?"

"He's the one who pointed out the diary." Jack looked in the rearview mirror. It was the fourth time he'd done that.

Kiley said, "Is the dead guy *still* by her bedside, Jack?"

"I don't think so."

She swallowed hard and glanced into the rearview mirror herself. "He's in the back seat, isn't he?"

Jack nodded. Kiley hit the brakes, then she leaned close to Jack and whispered, "We *can't* take him to my place. The dead *love* my place. He'll want to move in."

"Or move *on*," he replied.

"Oh, *come on!*" She looked behind her at the empty back seat. Stuffing was coming out from between some of the thinner seams.

"Chris's theory says it might be easier to cross over from a place where others already have. Which means–"

"Ah, hell." She closed her eyes, then opened them and turned around fully in order to address the empty back seat. "You're gonna fucking *love* my place. All the spooks do. But you can *not* stay. Got it? You try to stay beyond your welcome and I will fill the place to the rafters with exorcists and devil's dung! You reading me, spook?"

"It's okay, Kiley, he's gone."

"He's gone?" She looked at Jack again, then at the road. She'd come to a stop in the middle of a residential lane. Luckily, there was no traffic. She pushed out her bottom lip to blow her hair off her forehead. "You sure?"

He smiled then. First time he'd smiled all day, and she was relieved to see it. "Yeah," he said. "I'm sure." Then he shrugged. "I think you scared him."

CHAPTER FIVE

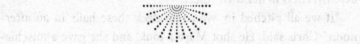

The gang had gathered in Kiley's living room with the pertinent items on the coffee table. The coat, the locket, and now, Rosalie's diary. Snacks and beverages found other perches around the room, to avoid accidents. The prearranged lunch had been pushed back to dinner in lieu of their visit to Rosalie Cantrell. So sad to see her lying there like that, forty-six and her life was over.

"This place needs a Christmas Tree," Maya said. "And I think you guys need it, too. You're almost as gloomy tonight as this house is."

Kiley got up from the rocking chair near the fireplace, which was dark and cold, but spotlessly clean. "I've been dying to decorate this place for Christmas. Things just seem to keep getting in the way."

"Since when do witches advocate for Christian holidays?" Johnny asked. He was teasing Maya, Kiley realized.

Maya rose to the bait. "The evergreen, the lights, the gifts were all part of Pagan observances of the Winter Solstice. Have you read *When Santa Was a Shaman*?"

"Why would I have read *When Santa Was a Shaman*?"

"It's pretty late, but there's still time," Chris interrupted, flagrantly trying to put the discussion back on track. "Decorations are still going up all over. People *need* Christmas this year, maybe more than ever. And this place sits here, gloomy as stale Halloween."

"I'm going to have it painted in the spring." Kiley heard the defensiveness in her own voice.

"If we all pitched in, we could deck these halls in an afternoon," Chris said. He shot Maya a look, and she gave a mischievous grinning nod. Then they were all looking at her, awaiting her answer. Apparently, one was required.

"Fine! Let's decorate." But she still didn't feel motivated.

Maya clapped her hands like she was sixteen instead of forty-whatever. Chris and Johnny high-fived across the sofa.

Jack said, "Can we please get back to the case now?" He leaned forward from his chair, to take Grandma Nisha's coat off the coffee table, and then lunged to his feet with kind of a weird yelp, dropped the coat to the door, and stared down at it in horror, saying, "What the hell? What the *hell?*"

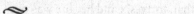

When Jack grabbed the coat, it felt cold, wet, sticky in his hands. He looked down and it was covered in mud and writhing with insects, centipedes and worms. He dropped it, and shouted something, staring at it in horror. But nobody said anything, and he looked up slowly to see them all just staring at him.

"You...don't see it?" he asked.

And then he looked at the coat again, and it was perfectly normal, as new as if it had just come off the department store mannequin yesterday, if yesterday was 1974. He crouched and picked it up again, watching it warily, in case it changed again.

"What did you see, Jack?" Johnny was standing by the fireplace holding a slice of pizza in one hand and a dinner plate in the other.

"Mud and maggots." Jack closed his eyes. "And rot. It was old. It looked like it had been …. Holy shit … it looked like it had been buried."

"Buried." Kiley repeated the word without inflection. Just dropped it. "Was anyone wearing it at the time?"

Jack shook his head, pressed one hand to his temple and paced the room. "Okay, okay, we have Grandma Nisha, who recently died, and who, I think, keeps sending us her coat. And we know it's her coat because we have a photo of her wearing it."

"But we also know she was not buried in it," Chris said. "Because she was cremated. It was in the obit, which I looked up last night."

"I wish we could find out what ever happened to that coat of hers," Kiley said. "You don't suppose the twins would know?"

"I'm writing it down." Maya slid out her phone and tapped rapidly.

"All right, all right." Jack stopped pacing, stared into the dark fireplace and wondered why he hadn't built a fire. The chimney had been inspected just before Kiley had bought the place. And Chris was right, the place was gloomy.

"And now we have another ghost," Kiley said, getting everyone's attention.

Jack said, "Yeah. A young man with matted, filthy hair and red and black face paint. We need to figure out who he is and how he's connected to Rosalie."

"Well, duh, Jack," Kiley said. And when he sent her a wounded look, she said, "Didn't Rosalie tell you who her ghost was when you treated her?"

"Treated her?" Chris said.

"Treated her how?" Maya asked.

Jack sighed. "I was going to tell you guys about this. Eventually. Um…" Everyone waited. Kiley wasn't even sure they were breathing. "I used to be a shrink. Rosalie was my patient for a short time right before she tried to kill herself. She said she was haunted by a ghost. I didn't believe her."

"It was before you knew," Johnny said softly. "Damn, Jack, I'm sorry."

"So that's why her mother came here, to you," Maya said. "Who did she tell you her ghost was, when you treated her?"

"Her first love. That's what she said. A boy from high school. That's all she ever told me."

Maya picked up the diary, started flipping pages, then stopped suddenly, and looked up from the book. "There are pages missing." She held the book up, open, revealing a half-inch worth of neat edges. The pages had been sliced by something razor sharp.

"Who would've done that?" Kiley asked. "Not the twins. They said they'd never had a key to the jewelry box."

"Rosalie herself?" Maya asked. "The diary is old, from her youth. She didn't try to take her life until five years ago. She certainly had time."

"We should read what's still there…" Kiley said.

"I volunteer." Maya slid the book into her handbag when Jack gave her a nod.

"So you saw Rosalie's ghost?" Johnny asked.

Jack nodded. "Yeah, for the first time. I didn't see it before, when I was treating her. I wish I had."

Johnny nodded slowly. "You did the best you could do at the time, Jack. I don't know you well, but I think I know that much."

Kiley thought he was pretty mature for a twenty-nine.

"I'd like to see Rosalie," Johnny said. "Sit with her, if I could."

"Why?" Jack asked.

Johnny was quiet for a second, looking at each of them in turn. And then he said, "I can speak to the dying. I've been able to since I was little. My grandfather, he's the only one I've ever told."

"Holy shit," Kiley said.

"Maybe I can speak to her soul, and she can tell us more about her ghost and her mother."

"The twins will never stand for it," Kiley said. And while Jack was nodding in agreement, she went on. "So you're gonna have to go in while they're distracted somewhere else."

"Whoa, whoa," Jack said. "That's breaking and entering...or something."

"Pssh. Not the way we're gonna do it." Kiley leaned forward in her chair, elbows on her knees. "Okay, okay, listen up. I think I have a plan."

When Jack arrived at the The Magic Shop the next morning, carrying a Box o' Joe and two dozen donuts from Dunkin, Chris had already unlocked the door and flipped the sign to OPEN. He saw Jack coming, and opened the door. Bells jingled and Jack smiled. He loved that sound. He loved his little shop. It was funny how he used to see it as a kind of helpful scam. He'd been feeding peoples' fantasies while giving them something to hang hope on for fun and profit. But now...

He was a true believer. The kind he used to make fun of. Maya's stuff was as real as his own, he'd seen it. And now this thing with Johnny thinking he could talk to Rosalie's soul—and Jack didn't even doubt he could do it. How could he doubt, when he could see dead people?

His own stuff wasn't fun. It was creepy and he didn't much like it. He'd have preferred ESP or telekinesis to mud and maggots and dead people showing up out of nowhere.

Chris had set up a folding table in the middle of the shop, white tablecloth with bright red and green holly leaves and berries bordering its edges. Jack put the coffee box there with its spout over the edge, and Chris took the boxes of donuts from him and used tongs to unload each pastry onto paper-lined tray.

"My grandma gave me all her Christmas decorations when she retired to Boca," Chris said. "Way too many for the apartment, so they're yours. They're taking up both my closets and all the space under my bed." He glanced upward as he said it, his apartment being the second story of the shop. "We can load them into your van later."

"Hold on, hold on, who said Kiley wanted two closets and a bed's worth of decorations?"

"She has room. I don't, and besides, she said she'd take them."

"Yeah, but she didn't know—"

"It's gonna be nice to have a place to hang up my clothes again." Chris walked away whistling "Deck the Halls."

Kiley was working remotely the next day, and having trouble focusing on her assignment. The Burnt Hills Gazette was a small-town weekly newspaper, with only a handful of employees, so everyone had to cover several beats. Her Holiday Traditions Old and New piece was due in three days and she had nothing but the title and a blinking cursor.

Her ass was on the sofa, her notebook on her lap, and her feet were on the coffee table where that nasty coat had been last night. She made Jack take it in to the shop with him. He'd boxed it and put it in the back of his pickup where she suspected it would remain until they took it back to the Cantrell house later on. Although she was afraid it would just show up again and not stop until they figured out what Grandma Nisha wanted from them and did it.

She was glad for the sound of the doorbell. Without even stopping to worry that it might be the walking coat, she set her laptop aside and went to the door.

Maya stood there smiling, a very large box in her hands. "Hi! I thought since it's lunch time, I wouldn't be interrupting your work day."

"It's lunch time? Thank God - er, Goddess. I need a break. Come on in." She swung the door wider and Maya carried her box inside. "I brought you my mantle decor from last year. I upgraded this year, and you have this gorgeous mantle sitting here almost naked." She set the box on the floor near the fireplace.

Oh, boy. They really were going to hold her to her promise to stop procrastinating and Christmas up the joint, weren't they? Maybe if she dove in, she could somehow instigate some holiday spirit. She just hadn't been feeling it so far this year.

"Knock yourself out. I'll order us some lunch. You want an Impossible Whopper?"

"Vegan style, please."

Kiley took her cell phone with her into the kitchen to place the order through her home delivery app and make them each a coffee.

"Is the coat here?" Maya called.

"I made Jack take it to the shop. I don't want it here. I don't want any of this here." She waited for her single cup brewer to churn out two mugs full, which was really four servings, because single cup brewers did not understand real world coffee mug sizes. Then she fixed Maya's the way she liked it—with the plant based-peppermint mocha latte creamer that she'd left in Kiley's fridge.

That's how regularly the Scoobs were meeting at her house to discuss ghost stuff—so regularly that Maya had left her favorite creamer in the fridge. God, was her place just destined to become Spook Central?

She supposed if you asked a passer-by that question, they'd take one look at it and nod with certainty. School kids walked on the opposite side of the road, sending terrified looks at the place.

It had been the scene of grisly murders. The restless dead had been buried there for years.

She added sugar to her own brew and carried both back into the living room.

And then she stopped as warmth pooled in her belly. The mantle was lined with pine-and-pine-cone garland with tiny fairy lights. It bordered a gathering of ceramic woodland creatures in wintry scenes, a reindeer with magnificent antlers on which a bright red cardinal perched, a family of polar bears. Two old-fashioned metal lanterns bracketed the scene, lit by pine-scented candles.

"Holy crap, Maya, you should do this for a living."

"I'm an influencer. Magical holiday decorating is one of my things."

"Magical?"

"Mm-hm. Anything you do can be magical. In this case, we're magically changing the energy of this house from a low vibration to a high one. You felt it when you walked into the room. I saw your face light up."

"It's true. I went from gloom to grin in zero-point-two seconds," Kiley said, smiling. "Can those lights twinkle?"

Maya raised her hand, and the lights began to twinkle.

Kiley gaped at her. "Wait a min– Did you ju–"

"I'm not *that* good." Maya turned her hand around. She was holding a small remote. "But I *did* have you going."

"You did." Laughing, Kiley handed her a mug and they sat in matching chairs, angled for the best view of the fireplace. "So raising the vibe of the place," Kiley said. "You think that could chase the ghosts away?"

"Positive energy repels negative energy," she said. "Like opposite sides of a magnet."

"Jack and I set wards around the four corners of the property. Onyx stones and stinky herbs from Jack's shop. We used your book, actually. I don't see that it's helped, no offense."

"Yeah, keeping things away from a place they're drawn to is a tough order. Filling the place with the opposite energy is easier. It makes them *want* to stay away." She shrugged. "Or it just pisses them off. Either way, it's uncomfortable as hell to be around opposing energies."

"And what happens if it just pisses them off?"

The doorbell cranked with its slightly discordant jangle. Could you have a doorbell tuned?

Before she could get it, the door opened a crack, and Johnny leaned in. "I brought some firewood and kindling. I'll pile it here beside the porch if that's okay with you."

"Wow. How do I rate all this special treatment?"

"I could see you longing for a fire last night and I thought– Oh. Hey, Maya."

"Hi, Johnny."

Wait, was Maya blushing?

Johnny cleared his throat, refocused on Kiley. "I thought a fire would be good. Fill the place with light. Fire cleanses. Purifies. Warms." Then he noticed the fireplace mantel and his face changed. It relaxed into a smile. "That looks amazing."

"Thanks," she and Maya said at the same time. Maya giggled. She actually *giggled*.

"You uh- want to stay for lunch, Johnny?" Kiley held up her phone. "I can add another meal to our takeout order."

"No, thanks. I have to get back to work. I just wanted to let you know what I was doing out here."

"Okay. Well, thanks. That was awesome of you."

"It's that time of year."

"See you tonight," Maya said.

"Seven sharp for my first felony. I'll be there." Johnny winked. He actually *winked*. Then he pulled the door closed. He'd held it open so long they'd need to burn all his firewood to warm the place up again.

CHAPTER SIX

*J*ack had bought the used Chevy Van for hauling stock he found at trade shows and sold at community fairs. Johnny, Maya, and Chris were in the back, where there was only one seat and a lot of cargo space. Kiley was in the passenger seat beside him. He thought she was excited. He thought she was insane. He was nervous as hell as he pulled over onto the shoulder of the road. It was rural-side-of suburban neighborhood, with no other houses close by, and woodlot across the street.

"We all know the plan. There's no reason this shouldn't go off without a hitch." Jack wondered if he was trying convince them or himself. "Just get in, do what you do, and get out. We won't be able to distract them long. They don't like us and they don't trust us."

"Fuck them, it's mutual." Kiley looked into the back. "We good?"

"We're good. I don't like it, but we're good," Johnny said.

"Okay, let's do it." Jack opened his door and got out. Kiley came around the van and they crossed the street together and walked up the driveway to the Cantrell House.

"This place makes me more eager to get my place painted in the spring," she said, "I wonder what it will cost."

"Thousands," Jack said. "We should do it ourselves."

She sent him a look that meant something and had him reviewing what he'd said in his mind. Did she think he was one of those guys who thought he could tackle jobs beyond his ability? "I painted houses to pay my way through med school. I know what I'm doing."

"I don't doubt you know what you're doing. Did I look doubtful to you?"

He shook his head. She rang the doorbell, an electric one with beautiful chimes you could hear from outside. Seconds ticked past before it opened, and Sara stood there. "I don't know how you're doing this, but the next time, I'm calling the police."

"The only thing we're doing is returning the coat again," Jack said. "And asking for ten minutes of your time. If you'll let us in."

"Why?"

"Because…I think your grandmother left something undone, and I don't think she's going to leave us alone until we do it."

"Bullshit. You're after money. You're a scam artist. You–"

"Let them in, Sara." Her brother came into view. "They're right. Grandma Nisha is uneasy. I hear her every night, pacing in Mom's room."

"There is nobody *pacing* in Mom's–"

"What, you think *Mom's* getting up and walking around in there?" He had raised his voice just then, and it clearly shocked his sister.

Sure as hell shocked Jack. The guy had been the walking definition of soft-spoken up to now.

"You've heard it, too, I know you have." Kev moved past her, took hold of the door and opened it wider. "Come in. We can talk in the sunroom. This way."

He turned and walked deeper into the house. Jack hesitated because Sara was still standing there gaping, but not Kiley. She strode past Sara like she wasn't there. Lou Grant would say she had spunk. Unlike Lou, Jack liked spunk. He followed, sending a friendly look Sara's way and willing her to join them. She finally sighed and closed the door, which locked automatically, then followed the others. Jack reached behind him and flipped the lock open. Sara looked back over her shoulder at him. He smiled his most innocent smile and hurried to catch up.

They moved past the staircase, into a massive kitchen, and through a utility type room to a sun room lined in glass. It had probably been an enclosed back porch. The sun spilled in, heating the room naturally.

"This is *nice*," Kiley said. "Does it get too hot in the summer?"

"The windows self-tint and the tops are vented," Sara said. "I can text you the number of the installer if it will get this over with any faster. What do you want?"

Kev nodded toward wicker chairs with quilted cushions in floral patterns. A glass topped wicker table stood between them. The set was identical to the one on the front porch. Kiley sat and Kev sat. Jack remained standing until Sara sat down, too, pretending to have manners. Then he took the chair near Kiley's.

"What do you think is troubling our grandmother, Mr. McCain?" Kev asked.

"Besides the fact that our mother tried to kill herself while under your psychiatric care, he means." Sara's accusation stabbed deep, hitting bone so hard his teeth hurt.

"You think he doesn't feel like shit about that already, Sara?" Kiley asked. "It ended his career. How the fuck was he supposed to know the ghost she was seeing was real?"

"Real," she repeated the word like it tasted bad.

"Real?" Kev asked. "What do you mean?"

They were both looking at Jack. He sent Kiley a WTF glance. She shrugged and raised her eyebrows and said, "Tell them."

He took a deep breath, closed his eyes. "I didn't think there were any such things as ghosts when I was treating your mother. But since then, I've...seen things."

"What kinds of things?" Kev asked. He was leaning forward in his seat.

"Your grandmother, for one," Kiley blurted. "You all saw her, too."

"We saw a coat with no one in it fall to the floor," Sara said, but she averted her eyes, because she knew perfectly well it had been more than that.

"Jack saw the ghost who's been haunting your mother, too. It was in her room the other day." She didn't add that they thought it was probably their father. Rosalie's first love. They didn't want to plant ideas, and so they wouldn't tell them that until they knew for sure.

Kev got to his feet. He was more animated than Jack had ever seen him. But Sara remained seated. "Let me guess," she said. "You can exorcise this ghost for us for an exorbitant fee, and–"

"I don't want your money." Jack modulated his tone, didn't yell, but the effort at keeping it civil left a telltale reverberation in his vocal cords.

"We just would like to get your grandmother off our ass so we can enjoy the holidays," Kiley said.

"So you saw it, you say?" That was Kev. He was clearly the more open-minded of the two, and super curious about all of this.

"I did. It was–"

Something crashed to the floor from upstairs. Sara shot to her feet and ran before anyone else had even reacted. They all followed her back through the house and up the stairs, down the hall and into that room at the end, where Rosalie lay in her hospital bed, eyes open, head moving around. A photograph lay face up on the floor, Rosalie holding her twin newborns.

Jack didn't see Johnny or Maya anywhere, but there hadn't

been time for them to get downstairs and outside to the van where Chris waited. Sara had been like a rocket.

"I know somebody's up here," she said. She looked around the room all but baring her teeth. "Come out now, or I'll call the police."

The closet door creaked open. Johnny and Maya came out, hands up in front of them in "I surrender" poses.

"What the hell are you doing in my mother's room?"

Johnny took a step forward and opened his mouth, but Jack held up a hand. "They're with us. They thought they might be able to help."

"By breaking into my dying mother's bedroom? That's it. I am done with you people. I want you out of here now. And don't come back, you hear me? I'm getting a restraining order before the night is out!"

Kev put a hand on her shoulder. "What do you have there?" He asked.

Jack noticed that Maya was holding a book. An old photograph album much like the one the twins had brought to the shop.

Maya looked down at it, too. Her finger was inside, holding a spot. She said, "I was looking through her photos while Johnny tried to speak to her soul. I found this." She opened the album and touched a large, old print of three shirtless young men wearing black and red striped face paint.

Jack sucked in a breath and moved closer. "That's him, that's the ghost!" He pointed at the guy on the right and took in every detail of the photo. It had been taken at a high school football game. There were bleachers and banners. He took the album and turned it toward the twins "Do you know who this is?"

"Of course we know who it is. It's our father." Sara rolled her eyes.

"He disappeared before we were born," Kev said.

"He walked out on his pregnant, teenage girlfriend and never looked back, to state it a little more clearly." Sara went to the bedside and smoothed her mother's hair. "It's okay. You're okay. We're here, Mom. Everything's okay."

Her demeanor had changed like a light switch, leaving Jack a little stunned. And both were genuine. Nothing put on with her.

Kev watched the two of them. "They were going to elope. He promised to come for her on the Christmas Eve before we were born. But he never came."

"Mom couldn't accept it," Sara continued. "That's when the delusions started. She convinced herself something had happened to him, that it was all part of some big mystery, that people were covering up the truth. And then she started seeing his ghost, and it just..."

Jack pulled a notepad from his pocket in which he'd sketched the ghost he'd seen by Rosalie's bed the other day. He flipped to the page, and then showed it to Sara. "This is the guy I saw by your mother's bed the other day. He's still there." He tilted his head toward the form at Rosalie's bedside. He just lingered there, gazing at her, eyes radiating sadness.

"Are you trying to say he really *is* dead?" Kev asked, incredulous.

Jack nodded solemnly. "Yeah. He's probably been dead the whole time. We can find out for sure, no charge, if you would tell us his name."

Kev wanted to answer, Jack could see that he did. But he looked at his sister instead.

"Yes. All right. Gabriel York," Sara said. "I have his birthday written down somewhere." She'd apparently decided not to have them arrested.

"Neither of you have ever tried to find him?" Kiley asked.

"Why would we? He didn't want us," Kev said. "That's what Grandma Nisha always said, anyway. Now...now I wonder." He looked at Johnny. "She said you were trying to...talk to her soul?"

"Feel her, really."

"And what did you...feel?"

"Honestly, Kev–" Sara bit off the rest when Kev held up a stop-sign hand, Jack thought more out of surprise than obedience.

"It wasn't hard," Johnny said. "Her entire focus is singularly on her love. She can't leave this life without him."

As Johnny spoke the words, the ghost turned and looked at him. For a moment, Jack was captivated by the stark pain in its eyes. And then those eyes shifted, and met his, and locked on. Jack turned his gaze away, but it was too late. He'd established contact for sure this time.

The ghostly mouth opened so wide it became the entire face and it roared its fury to the room. Jack was physically blasted backward, arms flying wide, heels dragging the floor until he smashed into the wall behind him and a picture fell and hit him in the head.

Kiley was by his side instantly, kneeling, touching, asking if he was okay.

Just as fast, Johnny and Maya had closed ranks in front of him, facing the bed, crouching in defensive postures that said they would fight whatever had just attacked him.

Between them and the bed, Sara and Kev were wide-eyed and terrified.

"I don't think it likes us here," Kiley said, kind of spotting Jack while he got to his feet. Holding his arm in hers, she pointed at where Jack was looking and said, "The feeling is mutual, ghost. I'll stay out of your place, and you'll stay out of mine. Got it? My house is off limits. OFF. LIMITS. And so is my man!"

Then she inclined her head toward the bedroom door, silently telling Johnny and Maya to get out. They did, exchanging wide-eyed looks on the way. Kiley followed, pulling Jack along by his arm, but never turning her back on that bed, and never lowering her finger. As they backed out the door, she said it again. "Off limits!" And then she turned and ran for the stairs.

She didn't let go of Jack's arm, so he had no choice but to go with her.

~

Jack drove them all back to his shop where everyone had left their respective cars. Kiley appreciated that. She knew he was trying his best to keep all of this ghost busting stuff away from her place. She, however, was no longer convinced it was within his control. Even so, he kept checking the rearview mirror every few seconds all the way. In fact, it had started to make her nervous how often he checked it. She'd turned to look behind them, but had seen nothing unusual, just the gang in the back and normal traffic outside.

He pulled into the parking lot behind his shop, and they all got out, forming a little circle in the pool of a streetlight. The wind was crisp and heavy, the sky dark.

"Is everybody okay?" Maya asked, looking around and pausing on each face.

"Well, I missed the whole thing, so yeah. I'm good," Chris said. He'd been sulking as the others had filled him in on the excitement.

"Next spook confrontation, we promise to put you front and center," Jack promised.

Chris rolled his eyes. Johnny studied Jack's face. "You're the one who was attacked. Are you all right?"

"Yeah." Jack rubbed his left shoulder as if to make sure. "Yeah, all good."

"Kiley?"

"Fine. Pissed. But fine." She looked around the parking lot. "He just better not try anything like that again."

"Johnny?" Maya asked.

He met her eyes and nodded once. "I'll be okay after some sage. Rosalie's energy is...dark and kind of sticky. But it makes

60

sense it would be. She's holding onto life against every physical law, against the will of her own soul. It would be best for her to let go, to move on." He shook his head sadly, then raised his eyes to Maya's again. "You?"

"It was sad looking at the albums. There are photos of them together, teenagers, so young and full of promise. So in love. But almost never smiling. I snapped some of them with my phone in case there are clues I might not have noticed right away." She pulled out the phone and everyone leaned in close as she scrolled through photos of a young couple in hats and mittens, building a snowman and having a snowball fight, each event documented by a series of shots. Kiley wondered who the photog had been. They were great photos.

"Look, there are holiday decorations on the street lamps," she said. "I bet this was that same winter, before their final Christmas. He doesn't look to me like a guy getting ready to dump his girlfriend and run for the hills. How about you?"

"We need to find out what happened to him," Maya said.

"I'll get on the net tonight. See what there is on him," Chris said.

"And I'll call Lieutenant Mendosa at the PD," Kiley said. She was her contact there for news stories. "Maybe she can help me out from her end."

"Tomorrow, though," Jack said. "We have plans for tonight."

"We do?" Kiley asked.

"Yes. We do. If Chris wouldn't mind swapping vehicles for the night? Chris?"

"Sure, boss." Chris pulled his pickup keys from his pocket and tossed them to Jack, who caught them easily.

"We'll meet at lunch hour tomorrow to compare notes, all right?" Jack said.

"At Kiley's?" Chris asked.

"I was thinking the diner—"

"My place," Kiley interrupted Jack. He sent her a questioning

61

look but she smiled it away. "Noon. Bring food. I like when people bring me food."

"I'll bring enough for everybody," Maya piped up, and then she gave a witchy wink and headed for her car before anyone could object.

Johnny watched her go, and Kiley watched Johnny watch her go, and tilted her head little bit. But then Jack was heading for the pickup with a sort of eagerness that didn't fit with the night they'd just had.

CHAPTER SEVEN

*J*ack pulled the pickup to a stop at a Christmas Tree farm. Rows and rows of pine and spruce bristled in every direction, and beyond them a lake as still and shining as peace itself. They pulled into the little half-circle driveway. A wood-structure stood behind it, wearing handmade wreaths as siding. It was a cut-your-own type tree farm, but there was a selection of pre-cut trees leaning up against one side of the building.

"You're taking me to get a Christmas tree?" Kiley asked.

Jack glanced at her before replying, tried to read her face. Her tone had been off. It wasn't like, "Awwww, you're taking me to get a Christmas tree," but more like, "What the actual hell are you taking me to get a Christmas tree for, you sappy fuck?" Her face told him nothing. She was amazing at poker. So he went, "Psssh, no. Not when you say it like *that*. I need a tree for the shop, you said you wanted one for the house, so... " He gave a careless, palms-up shrug. "You want to leave, just say so."

She bit her inner lip, like when you're either trying not to grin, or trying not to cry. Why was she so hard to read? Wasn't he supposedly gifted?

"I don't wanna leave."

He opened the door and got out, hoping his knees would hold him, being so weak with relief. She got out, too. Oversized bulbs looped from one ten-foot pole to the next, all around the lot. He headed for the trees, and she hurried up to join him, picking a random row that looked good. They passed a fencepost with several saws hanging from nails. He looked them over, like he knew which saw was best for cutting a Christmas tree. He'd never cut his own tree in his life. But he knew how to pick them. So he picked a saw like a boss and hoped for the best.

"What do you look for in a Christmas tree, generally speaking?" Kiley was turning left and right, as if trying to take them all in.

"What, you never had one before?"

"I was raised on artificial. Best money could buy." She'd inherited her family's fortune when their plane had gone down, then promptly lost it all to a con man. All she had left was the house she'd bought on a whim. And that had turned out to be haunted. Jack reminded himself that was probably a big reason why the place meant so much to her. It represented the last of what her parents had left her.

"Depends on what you like, I guess," he said. "My grandma McCain always liked long, soft needles. My mom wanted short needles but it had to be full. No bare spots. She liked blue spruce best. That's what these are, here. Smell." He ran his palm over a branch, and she leaned in to sniff.

"Smells like the Christmas potpourri Mom had all over the house this time of year." She sniffed again. "No, it smells better."

"Way better."

"Has cleansing properties, too," Kiley said. "Pine and spruce vibrate quite high. Whatever the fuck that means. Maya says negative ghosts can't hang out around positive vibes, so I'm all for that." She walked slowly ahead, moving around one tree, and then another. "How tall can I go, do you think? I'm terrible at judging height. My living room ceiling is twelve feet, I think."

He looked around, found a tree he thought was close, and pointed.

"That's smaller than I thought."

"Well, you have to leave a little room to put a star or angel or whatever on top. But we can always prune it a little. So there's some leeway in the—"

"Found it."

Her voice came from farther away than she'd been a second ago, and he followed it to a tree that was perfect in every way. "You have a good eye. Would it be sexist of me to offer to cut it for you?"

"It's either you or the tree-keeper, pal, cause *I'm* not cutting it."

He dropped down to crawl underneath the boughs and started sawing. The base seemed like it might be too big for an ordinary tree stand. It took a while to saw through it. He was still sawing when Gabriel York's face popped out of the limbs in front of him, eyes bulging and boring into his. He yelped and jerked backward. The tree fell over, and he dropped the saw.

"You okay?" Kiley asked. Again, her voice came from further away than he thought it should. She was standing beside the prettiest little Scotch pine you could ever see.

"Yeah, I… um… Squirrel." He looked around. No sign of Gabriel York.

"Squirrel?" She laughed and he went soft inside, then cussed himself out for being so much more into her than she was into him. Whatever. It was what it was.

"I think this one for the shop. Don't you?" she said, nodding at the pine. "Your grandmother would love it."

She *would* love it. She *did* love it. He felt it right to his toes, and because of all the ghosts in his life, he knew that was her, he was feeling. He supposed having this ability wasn't entirely bad. It was kind of comforting, in a way, to be utterly without any doubt that life goes on without the body.

He looked down, spotted the saw, and bent to pick it up. Then he took hold of a lower bough and began dragging Kiley's gigantic tree over to where she stood. He handed her the saw, and kept on going.

"Oh, come on, you don't expect me to–"

"It's your turn. Besides, that's a little guy."

"You suck, McCain." She knelt down, moved the saw back and forth way more times than should have been necessary, and then shouted "Timber!" As the thing slow-mo tilted to the right and stopped anticlimactically as soon as a lower limb touched down.

He laughed out loud. He couldn't even help it.

Kiley blew a curl off her forehead, picked up the three-foot tree, and carried it out before her like Liberty's torch.

Jack bought the trees, and two wreaths they'd been unable to resist, and put them all into the bed of Chris's pickup. As he drove them back to Kiley's, he worried. If Gabriel York had followed him to the tree lot, what was to stop him from following him back to Kiley's? She didn't want that. He didn't want to blow what they had by dragging ghosts to her door.

Then again, it was highly unlikely the ghost was following his physical trail. It had got a whiff of his energy. It could probably find him anywhere.

He knew that for sure when he pulled into Kiley's driveway and the ghost of a teenage boy standing at her door.

Jack got the tree out of the back and carried it to the front door, looking around for Gabriel, but he'd vanished. The hair on the back of Jack's neck was bristling, though. And that meant he was still nearby.

"No old lady in a coat, sans old lady," Kiley said. She ran past him, unlocked the door and went inside. Rubbing her arms, she said, "I'm gonna have to break down and turn on the furnace. It's getting downright chilly at night," and flipped on the light switch. Nothing happened.

"Well, that's weird." She turned it off and on again.

Something was wrong, Jack felt it in his bones. "Kiley, why don't you come out here, and let me–"

"Dude, I just sawed down a tree. You don't have to be the big strong guy when the lights go out." He still held the blue spruce by a low limb, pulling it along behind him up the porch steps. Kiley took out her phone, activated the flashlight, aimed it ahead of her and directly into the twisted, grimacing, dead face of Gabriel York. It shrieked at her, she screamed in terror, threw her phone at the ghost, pivoted and ran. Then Jack shrieked because she kneed him in the balls on her way over and through him. In 0.6 seconds, she was back in the truck

Jack got up. The tree lay cockeyed on the stairs behind him. Brushing needles off his coat sleeves, he went back up the steps and looked inside, but he didn't see anything. He reached around and flipped the lights. They came on, so he went the rest of the way in.

Turning back toward the open door and Kiley, he called, "I think he's gone."

The pickup door opened. "Make sure!" The pickup door slammed.

He turned on the outside lights for her, then went through the living room, dining room, kitchen, turning on every light and lamp along the way. It was a really nice place. So many unique touches. The original woodwork was all engraved with curls and swirls. In the dining room, there were hardwood valances on the tall windows, so intricately carved they were works of art, really. The cabinets were not mass produced. Tongue and groove boards painted white, bearing china knobs with pink roses, all crackled with age.

When he finished with the ground floor, he went upstairs, turning on the hall lights, the bedroom lights, the bathroom lights, all the lights. There was no sign of Gabriel, and the hair on his neck was once again, lying still. He could feel the ghost's absence as clearly as its presences. His talents, it seemed, were getting stronger.

He returned to the still-open front door and leaned out.

Kiley was in the passenger side, knees up, phone in front of her face.

"I'm not seeing anything," he said. "Not feeling anything, either."

The night was so cold and so quiet that he heard the creak when she rolled the window down. "Maya says we should get the tree up and decorate the hell out of it. Light drives out darkness, she says. So I overnighted a few things from the 'Zon, just now. We're gonna need a ladder."

"We are, huh?" He loved that she'd said "we."

She cranked the window back up before she got out of the truck. Then up came the pointy finger. "Listen up Gabriel York, we are ON this. You do *not* need to get our attention, you have it. We're going to find out what happened to you, so you just shut the fuck up and stay out of my house. One more act like that and we're off the case. You can stay earthbound forever. You hear me?"

Hand to God, the lights flickered.

"Yeah, you'd better." She hooked her thumbs through her belt loops and strode up the front steps, across the porch, and straight through the door Jack was holding open, pausing midway, almost chest to chest with him. "Let's do this."

"Hell, yes," he said, and he pulled the door closed.

She shot him a look. "Get the tree."

"Yeah, the tree. Right." Having revised his interpretation of *let's do this,* he headed back out and dragged the tree in. "You have a tree stand?"

"I have a five-gallon bucket and enough rocks to fill it, and about five boxes of decorations from Chris's mother."

"I think the bucket is brilliant. We'll need to trim off some of the lower branches. Let's get some drop cloths on this floor. This is probably the original old hardwood. We don't want evergreen sap all over that."

She met his eyes, and he realized he'd said "we" that time, and wished he could take it back. But she said, "You like my house."

"Well, yeah, I like your house. What, you thought I didn't?"

She shrugged one shoulder. "You never said. And you know, after it tried to kill you that time, I figured—"

"We fixed that. And this place is amazing. I'm sorry I never said so before. It's one of a kind. I think those china rose cupboard knobs might be original, too."

"I thought so, too!" She was smiling at him in a different way.

Maybe his romantic boyfriend gesture thing hadn't been a swing and a miss after all.

Kiley said, "Alexa, play Christmas music."

The machine complied. Then she started going through the boxes. "Oooh, candles. Mmmm. Very Christmassy." He heard her moving around the room as he sawed off the lower limbs, leveled the bottom of the tree, and finally placed it in the bucket, filling the space around it with rocks until it stood fairly straight.

"Which side facing front?"

Kiley appeared at his side with a glass of wine in her hand, which she placed into his. She sipped from her own and walked slowly around the tree, which was still out in the middle of the room. He stepped back while she did. She'd turned on the lights on her designed-by-Maya mantle, and had wadded up a bunch of newspapers and stuffed them into the fireplace, beneath artfully arranged kindling.

"This side is the front," she said, holding her arms out as if she were about to give the tree a hug. "We should get the lights on before we push it into the corner, don't you think?"

"I think that's brilliant. And I'm stoked we get to have a fire."

"Chestnuts roasting on an open fire," Alexa sang, and they both laughed.

"We get to have a fire *if* you bring in the wood. Johnny stacked some outside yesterday."

"Johnny brought you firewood?"

"Mm-hm."

"Should I be worried?"

She grinned. "Actually, I keep thinking there's a vibe between him and Maya."

"Maya has to be ten years—"

"Fifteen. Still." She shrugged. "We should test these lights. But I feel like we need snacks, first."

"I feel like we need a fire, first."

"You do the latter, and I'll do the former." She walked away toward her kitchen, singing along with The Christmas Song, and he fell a little bit harder. His romantic boyfriend gesture might've worked better on him than it had on her, because he was feeling awfully warm and fuzzy.

An hour later, they sat on the sofa with their feet up, a crackling fire on one side of the room, and a twinkling, decorated tree on the other.

"What kind of nasty ass ghost is gonna want to come in here now?" Kiley asked softly, and tinked her wine glass to his.

"No kind, that's what kind."

She dropped her head onto his shoulder. "Okay, so... I like it better when you're here than when you're not," she said, and then she bounced to her feet and said, "Let's go to bed."

And she was off, up the stairs and out of sight, and he was sitting there wondering what had just happened. Did she just sort of hint that they should maybe live together? Again? Only at her place, this time?

Were they ready? Was he ready?

"Ja-aaack," she called. "I'm naked up here."

He sprang off the couch and took the stairs two at a time, peeling his shirt over his head on the way,

CHAPTER EIGHT

*M*aya arrived at noon on the button, bearing a container filled with tin foil bundles Kiley hoped to God were her burritos, because her burritos were to die for.

She came in and looked around, nodding in approval. "The tree is gorgeous. And look at all the other holiday touches!"

Chris came in behind her with a shopping bag. "Aw, hey, my grandma's snowman village. And Rudolf!"

"You're getting those back when you have a house of your own," Kiley said.

"Nah, they look happy here. It's all good. Dang, I loved Rudolf."

"Everybody loves Rudolf," Jack said.

Kiley hid the grin that hearing him say that gave her and went to close the door, but Johnny arrived too, so she let him in. He had a pie. In a real pie tin. "Did you buy a pie and then put it in a pie tin so it would look like you baked it?" Kiley asked.

Johnny looked at her like she'd sprouted horns. "I baked it. I bake."

"I didn't know that about you. So you bake, and you can talk to the souls of the dying." Kiley was having fun getting to know these people. They'd been working cases together since Halloween. Only a few weeks, really. She'd started following Maya's vlog and was reading her book. Chris was a genius who was curious about everything and great with computers. He rented the apartment above Jack's shop. Johnny...she was still filling in the blanks about Johnny. But she was pretty sure he liked older women. Or at least one older woman.

She closed the door, and they all headed into the dining room to unload their food onto the already set table. Maya opened the lid on her bean burritos. Chris unloaded a canvas grocery bag. Salsa and vegan cheese shreds. That was more of Maya's food. He'd just carried it in, the brat.

Johnny set the pie on the table so it could make everyone's mouth water while they fed. Kiley sat down and helped herself to a foil wrapped burrito, still piping hot. "So, besides decorating the place, with plenty of lights, you'll notice—"

Everyone muttered some version of "it looks great."

"—I looked up exorcism rites. I used my press creds to get some university sourced stuff not available to the general public."

"Exorcism?" Chris asked.

"I figured if this Gabriel guy has attached himself to Rosalie, maybe we can pry his ass off. There are four different rites. There's a folder for each of you in the living room."

"You made folders?" Johnny asked.

"Well, yeah. Obviously."

Maya got up and ran into the living room, came back with one of the folders, already flipping pages before she sat down. "This is amazing material," she said. Then she looked up fast. "I get to keep this right? I mean, I'd consider it oathbound, if need be."

"Of course," Kiley said, and she shot a *what the hell is she talking about* eyebrow-raise at Jack, who replied with a *damned if I know* grimace-shrug.

Maya was already flipping pages again. "Yeah, this is going straight into the Book."

"You're writing another book?" Kiley asked.

"My Book of Shadows," she said, like Kiley would know what that was.

Chris said, "Gabriel York has been missing for twenty-five years. I've got every news story bookmarked. Sent them to all your phones."

Everyone started tapping their phones, reading in silence while eating, until Jack said, "Rosalie was the last person to hear from him that Christmas Eve. No reported sightings after that."

"So whatever happened, happened that night," Kiley said softly. She sighed. "While she was waiting for him, carrying his twin babies. Man, that's sad."

Maya laid her fork across her plate and leaned back in her chair. "I meditated with the coat, the last time we had possession of it, and then drew some tarot cards. Something unfinished. A need to cut away bonds. And then a waft of violent frustration swept the cards off the table, and I decided to let it go, for the moment."

"He was there? At your place?" Johnny asked, surging to his feet, then rather self-consciously sitting back down. "That's just… that's scary."

"It might've been him. Might've been Grandma Nisha," she said, head low, eyes not meeting anyone's.

She was a witch, Kiley thought. She wasn't supposed to get scared, was she? Or maybe that was a dumb stereotype.

"The coat was there, you said?" Chris asked.

"Yeah. I—"

"Wait, wait." He was tapping and then scrolling like mad. Then he started reading aloud. "'Spirits can attach themselves to people, places, or objects, and often to more than one of these at a time. Sometimes by choice, other times, against their own will, or apparently so, although it in truth, such a trap exists only for as long as the deceased believes it does. This is the case some-times in sudden, traumatic deaths. For example, a person in a car accident might become entangled with the car or maybe the loca-tion of the wreck. The murder victim might become bound with the weapon or person who killed him.'"

"Yeah, but...he probably wasn't killed by a coat," Jack said. "We don't even know for sure he was killed at all."

"He was declared legally dead ten years after he vanished," Chris said, then, to Kiley, "Did you get anything from your cop contacts?"

"I took the morning off."

"Hangover," Maya said.

"How the hell do you know that?"

She wiggled her fingers in that manner that's supposed to be spooky, and Johnny sort of choked on a laugh.

Kiley shrugged. "But yeah. You know, Christmas songs were playing and we were decorating and yada, yada, yada, wine's all gone and we're in bed til noon."

Chris looked from Kiley to Jack. "Wait, so you live here now?"

They both barked "No!" way too loudly. Then looked at each other. Kiley rolled her eyes, and shook her head and Jack dove into his burrito like his life depended on finishing it in three minutes or less.

Chris said, "The cop who was quoted in the paper was a rookie named Mendosa."

"Lieutenant Mendosa now. I know her," Kiley said. "She's going to be my first stop this afternoon. What else?"

"Excuse me a sec." Johnny got up and headed to the first-floor bathroom with one hand on his belly.

Maya sent a worried look after him, and Kiley said, "Is he okay?"

Maya widened her eyes. "Why are you asking me if he's okay? I have no idea."

"You think he's gonna finish his burrito?" Chris asked. His

76

own plate was clean.

Jack got up and started clearing plates.

"I'll make coffee and slice that pie," Kiley said.

"I can get it," Jack said. And then in quick-speak, "I mean, so you can show them your folders. Not like I'm the host here or anything. Just that I've already seen, because I was here and I collated and...stuff."

"I remember." She shrugged. "I mean, yeah, go ahead."

"Yeah?"

"Yeah, it's cool."

"Okay." He headed for the kitchen and Kiley stood there a minute, feeling like a thing had just happened. A step forward.

"This is great, Kiley," Chris said. He was in the living room, flipping through her folder from his usual chair, one of the two that bracketed the sofa. Jack would take the other one. Maya and Johnny would sit on the sofa. Kiley always took the rocking chair off to one side. She liked to move while she was thinking.

Johnny came back from the bathroom and sat on the couch.

"Some people don't handle my bean burritos so well," Maya said. She was on the other side of the sofa with her folder.

"I barely ate any," he said. "This was something else."

"Are you okay, though?" Kiley asked.

"Yeah. All good. Shoot me one of those folders of yours, huh?"

Chris leaned in to take one off the coffee table and tossed it to him like a Frisbee. Johnny clapped his hands and caught it between them. And then he smiled really wide, and said, "just like Rudy fecking Jarred," in what sounded like a British accent.

Everybody looked at him, then at each other. "Who's Rudy Jarred?" Maya asked.

Johnny blinked at her. "Who?"

Then Jack came in with two cups of coffee in each hand. He stopped. Then he looked at Johnny like the rest of them were as he lowered the mugs onto the table.

"You okay, Johnny?"

Johnny looked up and right into Jack's eyes. "Fine. Why?" Then he glanced at the coffee mugs and said, "I should get the pie," and headed back into the kitchen.

Jack said, "Chris, can you look up—"

"Rudy Jarred was a cricket player," Chris read from his phone. "Superstar."

"Cricket has superstars?" Kiley asked

"His career peaked twenty-five years ago. Which would be the year Gabriel York disappeared," Chris said. "We need to find out what happened to this guy. I think that's the key to everything."

Maya shook her head. "Are we not going to talk about what just happened to Johnny?"

Johnny chose that moment to re-enter the room with his own cup of coffee and a slice of pie dolloped with whipped cream. "What happened to Johnny?" he asked.

Maya lifted her brows and crossed her arms over her chest. "Johnny, who's Rudy Jarred?"

"Damned if I know. Does he have something to do with the case?"

"I'm gonna go get pie," Chris said on his way to the kitchen. "Anybody want pie?"

Maya put a hand on Johnny's shoulder. "Just a minute ago, Chris tossed you a folder, and you caught it and said, and I quote, 'just like Rudy feckin' Jarred.'" She put her own notion of a British accent on it, which was terrible.

Johnny looked around at the others, like she'd told a joke he didn't get and was wondering if any of them could explain the punchline. Only nobody was smiling.

"I don't remember doing that."

"We all saw it," Kiley said.

"Uh-uh." Jack held up a forefinger. "I didn't see it. I just walked in and saw everybody looking at you like you had lobsters crawling out of your ears. But I believe them. How much do you remember?"

Johnny dropped onto the sofa, leaning forward with his elbows on his knees. His long, dark hair curtained his face because his head was tipped down. "I remember up to, yeah, Chris throwing the folder. It felt like I caught it on auto-pilot. And then Jack was asking me if I was okay."

Chris returned with a couple plates of pie. She took one from him, noting the perfect way the fork was balanced, so it wouldn't fall, then sat down and said, "Be honest now, Johnny. Are you high right now?"

He lifted his head and grinned at her. "Not right now, no." And everyone laughed. The mood lightened decidedly. "I just zoned out. Brain fart, best way I can describe it. Maybe it's a line from a movie I saw, stuck in my brain."

"Maybe," Kiley said, and Jack nodded, and Chris even shrugged one shoulder. But Maya's eyes said, *no way.*

Kiley wheeled her way into a coffee date with Lieutenant Mendosa. It had to be fast, and close, she'd said, so Kiley met her at a cafe near the PD and chose an outdoor, socially distanced table. Normally these outdoor tables would've been gone by the end of September, but you know, life had changed.

Leaves skipped across the sidewalk, driven by a chilly breeze. A pot of coffee arrived with two cups, cream, and a pastel rainbow's worth of sweetener packets. She'd ordered a sampler platter of their most popular items in appetizer sizes. If Mendosa wanted it fast, Kiley could kiss up fast.

She was pouring her coffee into a diner mug twice as heavy as it looked, off white with two green stripes around the top, one thicker than the other, when Erica Mendosa pulled out a chair and sat down. She wore a natural Afro, dressy plaid pants with pencil slim legs that ended above the ankle, and a plain white button-down blouse with pleats to give it a touch of style. Her red felt pants-coat was unbuttoned, sash dangling. She carried no bag, but there was a bulging file folder with a fat rubber band around it under her arm. She dropped it onto the table, slid into her chair, and flipped over her coffee mug almost in a single motion.

Kiley poured, but her eyes kept darting to the folder. "Thanks for coming."

"Yeah, I don't have long."

"I know. I already ordered food."

Her brows went up. "You think you know what I want?"

"I got the sampler platter."

Mendosa blinked, sipped her coffee, closed her eyes blissfully. Yeah, it was good coffee. And then she said, "You're kind of smart, aren't you?"

"Kind of."

"Well, this is everything I have on York." She nodded at the bundle.

"I don't want you to get into any trouble—"

"I won't. I checked with the chief. He approved it."

Kiley frowned. "He approved it?"

The waitress arrived with their platter. Kiley moved the bundle off the table to make room for it. She'd expected to have to convince Mendosa to help her.

"Why was this so easy?" she asked.

"It's a cold case. No leads in years. If someone wants to help out, why the hell not?"

"So any aspiring Dick Tracy off the street who walked in could've had all this for the asking?"

Mendosa was spearing appetizers and loading them onto her plate. She demolished a jalapeño popper and a third of a dishful of queso dip, then said, "Tell you the truth, he's still pretty weirded out from the Miller case. He thinks you and that McCain character actually *have* something, you know?"

"Yeah?"

She nodded.

Kiley said, "It's all Jack. I don't... *have* anything. Except a house with an invisible 'Spooks Welcome' sign on its etheric lawn."

Mendosa shrugged. "You two think you've got something on this kid?"

"He's haunting us a little. Jack and me. Or maybe he's haunting an old lady's coat, and the old lady is haunting us. We don't know yet."

"Huh." She ate some more. Kiley did, too. As the selection on the platter dwindled, Mendosa wiped her mouth with a napkin, took a drink of coffee, which she had refilled, and leaned back in her chair. "He had no family, nobody to push for him. The case went cold. It shouldn't have. There was a pregnant girlfriend...I meant to look up her name—"

"Rosalie Cantrell."

"Yes. Yes. So you've found her?"

"Yeah."

"You talk to her yet? How'd she make out?"

"Had twins. She was sure Gabriel was dead, because she claimed his ghost was with her day and night. She wound up attempting suicide five years ago and has been in a persistent vegetative state ever since."

"Jesus." Mendosa looked horrified.

"Yeah."

"What happened to the kids?"

"Well, they were grown by then, but Rosalie was never stable. She never moved out of her mother's house. Is still there. The kids are okay, more or less. Inherited their grandmother's house and comatose mother."

"Wow. But they're okay?"

Kiley shrugged. "The brother's a nervous thing, keeps his head down, always looking at the floor. Sister's an overbearing, demanding jerk, but probably has good reason to be. To be honest, they've been less than helpful. But you know, they blame believing in ghosts for what happened to their mother, and so me, being kind of in the ghost biz…"

"I can see where that would be a problem."

"Besides, they weren't even born when Gabriel went missing. I don't think there's much they could tell us that might help."

"Well, I can only tell you what I remember. It was heart-breaking enough that it stuck with me. Gabriel York was only nineteen.."

"I'm surprised you remember anything."

"Hard case to forget. Nineteen-year-old kid disappears without a trace on Christmas Eve? Hell, you don't forget that. He was supposed to pick up his pregnant girlfriend. They were going to elope. But the girlfriend said he never arrived. She waited all night by her bedroom window, but he never came."

"They ever find his car?"

"Yeah. At the bus station. But since he hasn't been heard from in a couple'a decades, I don't really think he went traveling."

"Since he's been haunting his girlfriend for just as long, I don't think so, either."

"Never liked the girl's parents." Mendosa grabbed the final breadstick as she slid out of her chair.

"Why not?"

She shrugged. "Couldn't tell you. Maybe something in that file can."

"Thanks for this."

"Keep me posted," she said, pointing with the breadstick for emphasis, then she dipped it into a dish of salsa, bit off the end, and hurried away.

Kiley stacked their dishes atop the platter and moved it all aside so she could open the folder. And the first thing she saw was a photo of Gabriel York. He had wild dark curls, brown eyes, thick lashes that made him look innocent and kind, not angry and dead.

CHAPTER NINE

Kiley sat on the floor, the file open in front of her, a glass of wine in her left hand. Jack had a roaring fire going. The tree was lit and the entire place smelled like Christmas. Maya sat on the sofa beside Johnny, reading over his shoulder from a book with old cloth binding in faded red. Chris was in one of the soft chairs, tapping non-stop on his iPad. "So the family lore is that the twins' father—"

"Gabriel York," Kiley said, holding up a five by seven head-shot. "This is him without his face paint."

"Johnny?" Jack prompted. And Kiley knew why. She'd seen the look that had crossed Johnny's face.

"What?"

"You looked like you recognized the guy," Jack said.

A little frown knit Johnny's brow. "Yeah, for a second, I thought I did. But no. Please, continue. Family lore…"

"Family lore is that Gabriel York wanted to marry Rosalie, but that her father didn't approve. So they were going to elope on Christmas Eve. She waited for him, but he never came. And no one ever heard from him again."

"Rosalie's father," Maya said slowly. "We haven't talked about him much, have we?"

"Because he's been dead for a while," Kiley said.

"Yeah, but how long a while?" Chris tapped the screen as he spoke the name. "Edward O'Reilly Cantrell.".

Kiley flipped pages in the police file. "It's right here, I just saw it. Yes, right here. A statement from Grandma Nisha herself. "Edward and I had a falling out we just couldn't get past. He took his car and left us on December twenty-first. I remember because it was the winter solstice. The darkest night. My darkest, for sure.'" Kiley sighed heavily. "So first her husband vanishes without a trace…"

"And then her daughter's fiancé does the same a few days later?" Jack said, completing her thought.

Maya rose from the sofa and moved to stare into the fire. "I wonder where they were going to go? Gabriel and Rosalie? They must've planned to go somewhere."

"Well, there's really only one place *to* go," Johnny said. But he said it in an odd accent. He walked around the sofa to put a hand on Maya's shoulder. "I'll make it nice. And we'll be safe. No one knows but Uncle Sammy and me."

Maya stared at his face and her eyes went really wide.

"G-Gabriel?"

He lifted his brows. "You're not Rosalie!" The words exploded from him with some sort of percussive force that sent Maya reeling backward. Kiley surged to her feet and broke her progress, taking a full body hit, then grabbing hold to steady her. Johnny collapsed in on himself like a deflated balloon.

Jack dove, shoving a sofa pillow under his head before it hit the corner of the hearthstone. Chris was on his feet, gaze jumping from one of them to the next. "What the hell, what the hell?"

"That wasn't Johnny," Maya said. She got her footing, eased

out of Kiley's grasp, and moved toward where he lay on the floor. "His eyes changed. They were darker. And his voice…"

Kiley returned to the file, its pages scattered. She found what she was looking for, all the same. "Gabriel York was raised in England, by his mother. She died when he was sixteen, and he came here to live with his Uncle Samuel York, his only living relative," Kiley said, nutshelling what she found on the pages describing the young man.

"So…he probably spoke with a British accent," Maya whispered. She was sitting on the hearthstone, her hand on Johnny's shoulder as he gradually came around.

Chris tapped his screen. "Gabriel was his only living relative and heir."

"Heir to what?" Jack asked.

Johnny was sitting up, looking around, asking what had happened quietly, beneath the ongoing conversation.

"Cross referencing public records with both their names and the dates—"

"There was a cabin," Johnny said.

"There was a cabin," Chris said, overlapping him. And then he added, "Holy shit, how did you know that, Johnny?"

Johnny looked at Maya. "How did I know that?"

"I think Gabriel York might've … possessed you for a few seconds. Your eyes were different, and you spoke with a British accent. It's not the first time, either." She looked at the others. "We need to address this, find a way to protect him—"

"What we need to do is find the cabin," Johnny said. He looked at Maya and then the others. "I feel it to my bones. It's important we go there."

"Then we'll go there."

Chris said, "It's way the hell north, up in the Adirondacks. I have an address."

"I have a metric shit ton of camping gear," Jack said.

Kiley raised her eyebrows at him. "How did I not know this?"

"Because I figured you'd peg me as some kind of survivalist instead of just a camping enthusiast."

"Well, duh. Oh course not. So where is all this gear? You have a bunker somewhere?"

"See?"

"What?"

"I have camping gear, too," Johnny said. "Should we gather it up and meet back here?"

"Let's gather it up on the way, Maya said. "And let's take multiple vehicles. I want my All Wheel Drive. Chris and Johnny can ride with me."

"We'll take the van," Jack said. "There's room for a lot of gear in the back, and it's full of gas."

"I'm texting you the GPS coordinates," Chris told Jack, whose phone bleeped before the kid had finished speaking.

They drove. They stopped for fast food — Burger King, so Maya could have a vegan option. Then they drove some more. It got dark, and road signs were few and far between. It was at that point of darkness where the mountains were purple silhouettes against the distant sky, visible only between gaps in the treeline.

"It's creepy way the fuck up here in the dark," Kiley said.

Jack tapped the phone to call Maya, who picked up right away. "We were just going to call you. What's our plan of action?"

"I don't know," Kiley said. "Get there and look for clues?" Then she added, "Johnny, what did you get out of Rosalie's soul or whatever? You never said."

Johnny's voice came quieter than Maya's had. "She's holding on by sheer will. Says she will not die and leave her beloved Gabe behind—it's Gabe, by the way. No one called him Gabriel."

"What makes her think he won't just go with her?" Kiley

asked. "I mean, couldn't that be why he's hanging around, waiting for her so they can go together?"

"No, no. He isn't choosing to stay. Rosalie thinks he's trapped," Johnny said.

"That tracks," Jack said. "Everything about him feels...just claustrophobically trapped, bound, like he's stuck in a strait-jacket. It's a sense of panicked suffocation, all the time."

"Jeeziz," Maya whispered.

"Okay, okay. Gabe is trapped, and it's damned unpleasant and that's why he's so freaking dickish all the time," Kiley said. "Got it."

"So we need to free Gabe," Jack said.

Nodding, Kiley went on. "Rosalie is lingering in a vegetative coma because she won't die without taking Gabe with her."

"And Grandma Nisha can't be at peace until her daughter finally is?" Chris asked. "I don't know. It seems to me that if something that simple could keep you from crossing over, all the dead would be hanging around waiting for loved ones."

"So again, we need to free Gabe to free Rosalie and we need to free Rosalie before Grandma Nisha will move on," Kiley said, because saying it out loud, it almost made sense.

"And we need to do it all by Christmas Eve," Johnny said.

"Um... how do you know that, Johnny?" Kiley asked, her eyes on Jack's profile while she awaited a reply from the other car.

"I don't know," Johnny said at length. "But I'm sure of it."

Mm-hmm. And do you know what happens if we miss that deadline?"

"One of us will die."

∽

"Tell me this isn't the place," Kiley said, hours later.

Jack was still driving because it was his van. Kiley was still in the passenger side. But now Chris, who'd joined them after the last rest stop, was crouching between them, watching the in-dash screen and the view through the windshield. The rest of the space in back was crammed full of gear, "just in case."

That's what Jack said when she asked him about all the crap he was loading. That it was "just in case."

"This is the place," Chris said, nodding at the bramble-and-vine-smothered cabin.

"It looks like it's been sitting untouched for a hundred years," Kiley said kind of softly, because the place seemed to warrant it. But maybe that was just because it was so very dark outside. Inky dark. It had density, this darkness. They'd driven deep into the Adirondacks, and were miles from the nearest...anything. They'd lost cell service a few miles back.

"If this is the last place Gabriel York was before he died, then it can't have been sitting here like this for more than twenty-five," Chris pointed out.

"Ah, hell." Jack pulled the van slowly into the only spot that looked roughly like a driveway, a barely discernible pattern where the tall weeds and grasses were thinner and formed a distinct rectangle.

Johnny and Maya crept along right behind them in Maya's hybrid Land Rover.

"I don't see any electric lines," Jack said. He stopped the van, shut it off, but left the headlights on. It wasn't even fully nighttime, dusk, maybe. But this place was dark all the same. There were gigantic, bare-limbed trees looming over it like angry old men trying to frighten it, and behind them, evergreens made a solid backdrop that admitted no light. The cabin wore a coat of briars and brambles and a skirt of thick weeds and saplings.

Jack reached into his door's side pocket and pulled out a heavy-looking metal flashlight as long as his forearm. Then he nodded at Kiley and said, "There's one on your side, too."

She reached down and found a flashlight. Hers was blue. His was red. She wanted to trade.

Chris flicked one on from behind, right into her eyes, then quickly away when she closed them and put up her hand.

Johnny and Maya were already out of their car, armed with flashlights of their own. Kiley inhaled and wrinkled her nose at the hint of decay that tinged the scent of the pines and the forest itself. The ground was squishy, so wet that it came up into her shoes. It had been a rainy summer in most of the state, though, and that was probably why it was so overgrown, anyway. Kiley reminded herself that a vine-covered cabin in the summer would be whimsical, not terrifying. It was just that it was winter and the brambles were leafless and brown, decked only by their thorns and withered, dried bits here and there, rasping loud in the cold breeze.

"It sounds like it's warning us away," she said. So much for trying to find a positive thought about the place.

They walked closer, Jack led the way, which was really impressive, Kiley thought, since she knew he was as scared as she was. He just hid it better.

She stuck close, holding her flashlight for dear life. They sort of crouched while they walked, almost in expectation of attack. Jack aimed his beam straight ahead, so she swung hers, making wide arcs, scanning the weeds and undergrowth around them, the forest beyond that. No glowing eyes. Something skittered away, shaking the grasses as her light moved over them. She thought her heart was going to pound through her chest and pressed a hand there to keep it contained.

Jack reached back, took her hand from her chest and held it in his. "Woodchuck. Rabbit. Raccoon. Something small and furry that would make you go 'aww' in the daytime."

"I do not go 'aww'."

Maya snort laughed behind her.

A little more relaxed, they started moving forward again. Jack aimed his light at the ground, found two front steps and swept them clear of litter with his foot. And then he tore vines away from the door, took hold of the knob and twisted it. "It's not locked. Swollen, though." He put his shoulder against it and pushed the door open.

Its hinges creaked like damned souls being dragged to hell. The sound only stopped when the door stood wide, and Jack was inside, shining his light around. He said, "Huh."

Which made Kiley look, too. She aimed the beam around. The place was dusty and there were cobwebs, but it was in good repair.

"I'll get some lights," Johnny said from the rear of the group. The rest of them fanned out, exploring the place by flashlight. Large front room. The few pieces of furniture—a sofa and a couple of chairs—were all sheet-draped. There was a nice cobble-stone fireplace that took up a whole wall. It had shelves built into it and a big slab of wood for a mantle. There were rooms off it, two on each side, and three of them had flashlight beams moving around inside.

Johnny came through the front door with two of those white-gas lanterns in each hand. He lined them up on the floor inside, and kneeling, began the process of lighting them, which seemed unnecessarily complicated. There was pumping involved. Kiley had no idea. But when the first one took, the light was tremendous and bright white. It glowed like a miniature sun.

"Oh, hell, I have to get one of those," she said. "You're going to have to show me how to work them, Johnny."

"Sure thing." He was already working on the second one. "If you find a place to hang it up high, it'll light the whole room."

Kiley shut off her flashlight, took the glowing lantern by its bail handle and, holding it up high, turned to shine it around the place. Then she stopped and took a stuttering breath. The others heard or sensed her reaction and turned to see what had caused it. There in the corner, was the skeleton of a Christmas tree. Not a needle still attached. But there were ornaments made of pine cones and sea-shells, and paper rings.

"He was going to bring her here," Maya whispered. "He put up a Christmas tree for her. Oh my God."

"Look, the fire was all laid out and ready," Chris said.

Kiley put the bright lantern up on the mantle. There was a wagon wheel hanging from the ceiling with a hook in the middle. The lantern should hang there, but she couldn't reach it.

Johnny rose with the second lantern glowing, and they moved toward the only room not currently being explored, which turned out to be the kitchen. There was an antique wood burning cook stove, a sink basin with a hand pump mounted just to one side over it. There were shelves, not cupboards, and in the middle, another wagon wheel with a hook in the center. Johnny hung the second lantern there.

Kiley went to the sink and started pumping the handle. It took about ten pumps before she heard a hopeful gurgle, and in three more, water flowed. She put her fingers in it, then brought them close to sniff. "You think the water's good?"

"I don't know," Jack said. "We brought enough so we shouldn't have to find out."

"Two bedrooms and a bathroom with a flushable toilet," Chris called, coming to join them in the kitchen. "You just have to dump the water down. There's a shower stall too. No idea if it works, or how it could, but it's in there."

They returned to the main room, which already bore a few boxes and crates. Maya had begun unloading her vehicle. Johnny said, "I'll get a fire going."

"I'm gonna find something to eat," Chris said, heading for the van.

"No, no, the hell with settling in," Kiley said. "Before we do anything else, we should comb this place for evidence. Any sign that Gabriel was ever here that night.

Jack nodded slow. "We should've brought the coat."

"No way should we have brought that coat here," Kiley said.

Maya looked at Johnny. He shrugged and said, "I brought the

coat." Everyone exclaimed or swore at him all at once, and he shrugged, palms up, and said, "What? I thought we came here to find out what happened? The coat is involved, somehow."

"The coat is haunted, Johnny," Maya said. "Or cursed or something."

"Let's get on with the search so we can settle in," Kiley said. "Inside tonight, outside tomorrow, all right? And for now, Johnny, leave the ghost coat in the car."

"Okay."

So they went through the house, with flashlights and lanterns. Kiley had even brought gloves and plastic bags. Maya was filming everything on her phone. The living room first, every inch of it. Chris was feeling along the top edge of door trim and looking behind picture frames. Johnny was taking the sheets, then the plastic that was under the sheets, and eventually the cushions off the furniture, and checking the cracks and crevices and underneath. He said, "I've got an earring."

"Don't touch it! Get this Maya," Kiley said, hurrying to him with her zipper bag. He took the bag, reached under the sofa, and used the bag to pick up the earring. When he pulled it out, he let it fall into the bottom of the bag and handed it over to Kiley.

It was a button-shaped glittery clip-on, made of numerous green glass crystals. "Vintage."

"Like the coat?" Johnny asked.

She nodded. "Exactly. Problem is you said nobody knew about this place but you and your uncle."

"Gabe and his uncle," Johnny corrected.

"Better bring the camera in here," Chris called from the bathroom. They all hurried in, Maya leading with her phone recording. The bathroom was well lit with one of the gas lanterns blazing, but Chris aimed his flashlight all the same, at a corner of the ceiling above the bathtub, where dark spatters were. Maya aimed the camera upward coming in close. "Get some stills, somebody."

"I'm on it," Kiley said, snapping closeups with her phone.

"Think it's blood?" Chris asked from out in the living room.

"Probably not," Jack said, also still outside the room. "But we're checking everything, so…"

"Yeah."

There was nothing notable in the rest of the house, except its emptiness. When they finished the search, they went ahead and unloaded their stuff. The bedrooms were bare, not a stick of furniture. Nothing in the closets but a few bare coat hangers. But Jack and Johnny had brought sleeping bags enough for all of them, and within short order they'd gathered in the living room. Kiley dug into the bagful of munchies she had brought along for the trip. Sweet Spicy Chili Doritos, Tostitos, Oreos, Fig Newtons, and a selection of salsas for dipping.

As she unpacked the snacks on the living room's coffee table, which was a slab of a tree under a gallon of shellac, Maya rose from her spot, and looked down at the selection, then up at Kiley. "Everything here is vegan."

"Yep. Super easy to find lists of vegan junk food on the net."

"Yeah, but nobody ever does." She crossed the boundary of the table between them and hugged her. A real hug, nice and close and firm. Kind of a big display for Kiley's taste, but it moved her just the same. She patted Maya's shoulders awkwardly until she was released, and took two steps backward.

"Shit," Johnny said. "I brought the makings for hoagies. In that cooler I brought."

"I brought my own foo– " Maya tripped to a stop. "Wait. You put *meat* in my car?"

"I'll get it out right now. Shit, Maya, I'm sorry." He ran outside, leaving the door open behind him. Maya shook her head and said, "You win some, you lose some. Thank Goddess I didn't accept his offer to put my cold things into his cooler of death. Jerk."

"He's young," Jack said. "He wasn't thinking."

"I think he has a crush on you," Kiley said.

"Aw, *man*." Chris blurted, then he sighed. "Yeah, I see it now."

Jack swung his head toward the door like he'd heard something. Kiley hadn't heard anything, but she looked, too.

"What's taking him so long?" Maya asked as Jack rose from the sofa and headed toward the door.

"Jack? What's going on?" Kiley followed him, touched his shoulder to get his attention, but he brushed her off and said, "Something's happening. Lock this place down, and stay inside."

"Wait!" Chris bolted in front of him before he reached the door, a walkie-talkie in one hand, flashlight in the other. "This is why you brought gear. Channel four on the radio, okay?"

Jack took the radio and turned it on as he moved past Chris, clapping his shoulder on the way. "Thanks for always looking out for me, kid."

"Somebody's gotta do it."

Jack went out the door and pulled it closed behind him.

CHAPTER TEN

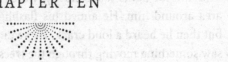

*J*ack had been antsy ever since he'd set eyes on the place. There was something bad there. It was like a rancid smell that hung in the air, but not a smell, exactly. It had him feeling nervous and buzzy, like after four cups of high-test coffee. His nerves were electrically charged and tingling.

He went down the two steps to the ground. It was really dark. No moonlight. The air was heavy and dank with that wet, earthy smell of fungus on rotting tree trunks. Beneath it, you could smell the pines when the breeze picked up. When it did, their boughs moved, allowing a glimpse of a star here and there. He scanned the darkness ahead of him, the van was illuminated a little bit by the cabin lights of Maya's hybrid. Its hatch was open, so the interior lights were on.

"Hey, Johnny," he called. "Where are you?"

No answer.

Jack kept moving, walked carefully around the van, shining his light inside, and seeing nothing. He checked behind it before stepping fully past, like there might be a boogie man waiting to jump out. Somewhere a lone grasshopper played his sad violin while winter breathed down his neck.

"Johnny!"

Jack checked inside Maya's vehicle. A white food cooler sat on the ground behind it car. He reached up and closed the hatch. The interior lights faded slowly, which made it easier to see the area around him. He aimed his flashlight, not seeing anything, but then he heard a loud crack. He swung the beam that way, and saw something moving through the trees.

"Johnny!" He headed into the woods, not even sure Johnny was what he'd seen. He ran several yards, then stopped to listen. Yes, for sure. Footsteps moving up ahead, beyond the reach of his flashlight beam. He hurried and eventually made out the shape of a person—of Johnny—striding though the forest. Moving even faster, he had to shine his light on the ground to keep from tripping over roots and rotting limbs, aiming it upward in short flicks to keep track of Johnny. He kept shouting Johnny's name, but it was no use.

"Dammit, Johnny, *stop!*"

Johnny stopped. But not because of Jack's shout. He stood perfectly still, looking left and right, as if getting his bearings. Then he started off again, angling left.

Jack hurried and finally, finally caught up. "What the hell, dude?" He grabbed Johnny's shoulder to turn him around, but Johnny's fist came around faster. It plowed Jack in the face and knocked him flat on his ass.

"I don't like this. I don't freaking like this," Kiley said.

"I don't, either." Maya unlocked the door and swung it open.

"Wait, wait," Chris said, putting a hand on her shoulder.

"Unless some of that crap you guys brought includes weapons, you better move your hand. I'm going."

"It does, actually."

They both looked at Chris. He gave his head a shake. "Not actual weapons, but there's a multi-tool–" As he spoke, he knelt near a pile of gear yet to be unpacked. "Foldable shovel, hunting knife–"

"Now we're talking. I'll take the knife." Maya took it right out of his hand, and headed for the door. Kiley grabbed the shovel, unfolded and locked it. It would make a great weapon. She just hoped she wouldn't need it.

"That leaves me the…" Chris held up the oversized pocket knife which held a sharp blade, a serrated blade, a can opener, a corkscrew, a bottle opener, and a partridge in a pear tree. He pried out one of the blades as the women headed out the door. Then he said, "Flashlights!"

Kiley let him catch up long enough to hand her a light like a baton in a relay race. Then she picked up her pace again. "Jack went into the woods over there," she said, aiming her beam and following the path it laid. A cricket chirped, but it sounded like it was playing on low speed. "I couldn't see him from the window after that. Just his light for a few yards, then nothing."

She slowed her pace as the forest closed in around her. The darkness felt alive, like it was watching their every move as it slowly swallowed them up. Her feet moved more slowly, and she aimed the beam ahead, then down. Leaves and pine cones crunched under every step, releasing a waft of fragrance, but not fresh and aromatic like in late September. This was December. This smell was decay.

"What's that?" Maya asked, coming up beside her.

Kiley followed the beam of her light to a shape on the ground and then Chris said, "Jack!" and shot past them both.

Jack was lying on his back on the ground. They all knelt around him, dropping their flashlights to the ground. Chris was checking for a pulse, and Kiley was using her sleeve to wipe the blood from his face.

He grimaced in pain before he opened his eyes. "What...?"

"Are you okay?" Kiley asked, helping him when he tried to sit up. "What happened?"

"Johnny decked me. Hell." He touched his nose, then looked at his fingers. "I'm okay, I'm okay. Help me up." Chris grabbed one arm and Kiley the other. He got up, gave his head a shake and looked around. "How long was I out? Did you see him?"

"Minutes," Maya said. Then she looked deeper into the woods. "Johnny! Johnny, where are you?"

"That's the way he was heading," Jack said, and he started in that direction with everyone following.

A scream of pure anguish rent the woods, spurring them to run headlong. Chris fell twice. Kiley got smacked in the face with branches. Maya weaved and bobbed like a feral woodland creature, and then they found him. Johnny was cowering against a tree trunk, arms up defensively, and his head was bleeding.

Maya didn't even slow down, just skidded to her knees near him, grabbed his shoulders, said his name, but he flung his arms outward and sent her flying away from him. She landed on her back, which made Kiley hesitate in her own approach. Jack moved past her, holding up his hands for calm.

"It's me, pal. It's Jack."

Johnny lifted his face. It was twisted up and wet with tears and blood, dripping from a deadly-looking gash in his forehead. "Whywhywhywhywhy?" he moaned. And then, "Please," all long and drawn out.

"John! Hey, snap out of it, come on, it's us. It's your friends. It's Jack and Kiley, Maya and Chris. Come on, Johnny, wake up."

"You're safe, Johnny. No one can hurt you here," Maya said. She'd picked herself up from the ground where he'd shoved her, brushed off her jeans and moved in close again. She stopped about two feet away and said, "Gabe?"

Johnny's head snapped toward her, and he said, "Rosalie?"

Then he passed out cold, sinking to the ground in the same curled up position.

"What the actual fuck?" Kiley demanded.

Maya crowded past them closer to Johnny. She drew a shape on his forehead with her finger and muttered words in a language Kiley had never heard before.

Jeezuz!" Jack backed up suddenly, eyes wide and fixed on Johnny. No, not quite on Johnny. "Did you see that? Tell me somebody saw that?" He searched each face.

Kiley shook her head, so did Chris. Maya said, "I didn't see it, but I see this." She wiped her hand right across the bloody gash in Johnny's head. But there was no gash. She wiped away the blood to reveal a smooth, uninjured forehead.

"What did you see, Jack?" Kiley asked and wished she hadn't. She really didn't want to know.

"What do I still see," he replied. "Gabe just ripped himself apart from Johnny. He's standing there four feet to the left."

"Get away!" Maya said, and she rapidly drew a shape in the air. In a flash of insight, Kiley realized it was a star. "You do not belong here. You must go through the western gate."

"It's moving toward him again," Jack said. "No!" He lunged closer and grabbed Johnny's hand, then Kiley's with the other. Maya, apparently reading his intent, grabbed Chris's hand in one and Johnny's in the other. Kiley and Chris joined hands, forming a circle and the second they did, Kiley saw the ghost.

Gabriel York was vaporous and his legs didn't reach the ground. He wore tattered, filthy clothes. His dark curls were matted, his face was smeared with mud and blood, and there was an angular cut in the right side of his forehead. Big and deep and black inside.

"Is everyone seeing this?" Kiley whispered, because she couldn't look away to check their eyes.

"I am," Maya said at the same time Chris said, "Yeah. Holy shit, yeah."

Gabe didn't look at them. He looked at Johnny, and as soon as he did, Maya shouted, "I conjure the Circle of Power! Arise! Surround! Protect!"

Gabe lunged toward Johnny, hit an invisible barrier, and shattered into a million wisps that vanished like sparks from a vampire. Moments later, he sort of reassembled a few feet away.

Maya raised her arms, and those of the hands she clasped, and everyone else did likewise. Gabe lowered his head, turned, and moved away into the darkness of the forest.

Kiley dropped straight down onto her knees and swore for a full minute. The wind was picking up, noisy in the tree tops. Jack bent close. "You okay? Can you walk back? Cause I don't think Chris is up to carrying Johnny."

Johnny chose that moment to open his eyes and mutter, "I can walk. What the hell happened? Why is my head hurting so bad?"

"You were possessed, again, pal," Jack said.

"And your head was split open," Chris added.

Johnny pressed his fingers to his head right where the hole had been. "Blood's still there. Gaping wound gone."

It was starting to rain.

Kiley let Jack help her to her feet while Chris clasped Johnny's hand and hauled him up onto his. They headed back through the woods with the rain and wind escalating at a concerning pace. Jack said, "We have to get back to the cabin."

"Cabin my ass" Kiley said. "We are going exactly as far as the vehicles and then we are driving the fuck out of here."

"I agree," Chris said. "To where, though?"

"The nearest internet signal, and after that the nearest motel." Kiley checked her pockets for keys, then swore. "We'll have to go inside for keys, so grab whatever is important. But screw the rest of the gear. We can come back in the morning."

They trudged out of the woods where the rain fell harder, and the wind blew so hard Kiley was knocked off balance and latched onto Jack's arm. "Is this *normal*? Can ghosts *do* this, Jack?"

"I've had my powers for a month and a half. How would I know?" They were following their own tire tracks through the weeds toward the cars.

"You've only *known* you've had 'em for a month and a half," Chris corrected.

Kiley held up a hand. "We can discuss this when we are out of here. Who wants to go inside?"

"We'll all go." Maya moved up beside her. "I think there's safety in numbers, so let's stick together."

"Good idea," Chris said. "We can all fit in the van—"

"We can all fit in the Land Rover," Maya said.

"I'm not leaving my van." Jack had pulled ahead of the rest of them and was almost to the front door.

Kiley caught up to him almost instantly, then realized the others had, too, and they were all so close they resembled a football huddle. Jack gave her a look and she said, "What? Maya said stick together."

So they went inside, together. Kiley headed right for the corner where she'd left her purse, snatched it up. Jack grabbed a big flashlight and his smallest backpack. Johnny took a small duffel. Kiley said, "Better grab dry clothes. We can change on the road." So everybody grabbed another bag, and then they ran out to the vehicles, through the pouring rain.

Jack jumped into the van's driver's side, and Kiley took the passenger side. The other three dove into the back where Chris offered the only seat to Johnny.

Johnny said, "The seat's for Maya."

"Why, cause I'm a girl?" and sat on the floor. Chris closed the back doors and Jack turned the key. He was rewarded with a *click-click.*

He looked at Kiley. She looked at him. He tried again.

Click click.

"Son of a—"

Jack wrenched open the door and got out of the van. The rain was coming down harder than ever, sideways in the slashing wind. He struggled to shut the door against its force, popped the hood and leaned over the engine, shining his phone's flashlight inside.

The others piled out of the back and Maya shouted full volume, "Come on! We'll just take the Land Rover."

Kiley got out as Maya started running toward her car.

There was a *crack* you could feel in your bones that came from everywhere at once. Kiley turned in time to see a tree falling toward Maya's car.

"Look out!"

The car was crushed. There were limbs everywhere, and she couldn't see Maya anymore.

CHAPTER ELEVEN

Jack said, "Bring the flashlights. All you can find."
Then he headed for the disaster while Kiley sprinted
inside. He aimed his light at the place where Johnny
was yanking limbs, snapping some of them right off. He ran to
him, hand to his shoulder, "Wait!"

Johnny yanked against his grip. "We have to get her out—"

"Listen, don't break off any limbs that are holding the tree up
off the ground! Understand? Nothing that's holding it up."

Johnny stopped fighting. "Right. Right, okay, good. You heard
that, Chris?"

"Got it," Chris called.

He was crawling underneath, and from the sounds, he'd made
his way pretty deep. Jack said, "Chris, don't get yourself trapped,
too."

"Wait, bring your light here," Johnny said. "Maya! Say
something."

She didn't. Kiley was back, slapping a flashlight into his hand
before Jack could, and Johnny aimed it. A lower leg was thrust
out from the limbs, jeans pushed up to the knee, scratches all
along the way.

"She's over here," Johnny yelled.

The tree trembled as Chris made his way back out.

"Take it easy," Jack said. "You're shaking the tree. Maya, hang on. We'll have you out of there a minute. Just hang on." She didn't respond, and he tried not to think she might be dead, but thought it anyway. He even looked for her, because if she were dead, no question she'd be hanging around her body out of curiosity, if nothing else. But he didn't see her spectral form.

He did see Gabe's, though. He stood near the woods, gazing at Jack so intently it seemed he had something to say. Something he was trying to get across just with that look.

Chris finally got clear of the fallen foliage and came to where they stood. He looked at the illuminated leg and said, "How are we gonna get her out of there?"

"You're gonna get her out of there," Jack told him.

"I am?"

"You're the brush-crawler." Jack moved to a good spot, crouched low enough to put his shoulders under the tree's trunk, which had to be two feet in diameter. At least it wasn't a conifer. He nodded to Johnny who got the message and found a spot further down, crouching even deeper than Jack was. "We lift, you get Maya," Jack said. "Ready?"

Chris dropped to hands and knees, flashlight in hand. Kiley moved under the tree next to Jack and put her hands on the tree trunk from beneath.

"Lift!" Jack said, and he pushed upward. He knew the others were too, because the tree moved. Not a lot, but then they pushed harder and it rose a little more. He couldn't watch Chris's progress, but he heard branches snapping and breaking.

And then suddenly, Chris yelled "Clear!"

"Slowly, now!" Together, Jack and Johnny lowered the tree back down until it was supporting its own weight, and then they got clear of it.

Chris stood in the pouring rain between the tree-crushed Land-Rover and the van, with Maya lying across his arms. Johnny got there first, scooped Maya from him and speed walked straight into the pitch-dark cabin. Jack, Kiley and Chris made it inside in time to hear him asking, "Will somebody light a lantern?"

"I'm on it," Chris said, hurrying away, rattling around.

"Put her on the sofa, Johnny." Kiley grabbed hold of the gigantic wood slab coffee table, and seemed surprised when it didn't budge. Then Jack grabbed the other side to help move it out of the way.

The lantern came to life. Chris carried it with him to the door and turned the lock against the storm and whatever other nasties might be out there howling with it.

"I thought the bedroom, where it's quieter," Johnny began. He still hadn't put Maya down.

"We stay together," Kiley said. Her tone had changed from friend to matriarch. "Sofa. *Now.*"

Johnny put Maya on the sofa, carefully laying her head on the padded arm for a pillow. "She's breathing," he said. "Her heartbeat feels strong."

Chris brought the light to the coffee table and set it there. Johnny ran his hands over Maya's face, and then her head, and then he stopped. "She was hit in the head. There's a lump, small cut."

"We have ice!" Kiley ran to the kitchen, where they'd put the ice chest full of food.

Johnny ran his hands over Maya's arms, then her legs. Then he took off her shoes. Jack observed it all, no longer in any doubt about Johnny's feelings for Maya. It was obvious. He met Chris's gaze and he nodded, as if to say, yeah, I see it, too.

Kiley came back with an ice pack and Johnny took it and laid it on Maya's injured head. "I don't know what else to do."

"We're icing it," Kiley said. "That's good. And we keep her

warm and elevate her feet or something, so she won't go into shock. That's a thing, right?

Chris walked to the foot of the couch and awkwardly lifted Maya's feet, clad in heavy socks, up onto the sofa's opposite arm. Jack went for a sleeping bag, unrolled and unzipped it, then laid it over her for a blanket.

"Someone should go for help," Chris said. "I'll do it. I'm pretty fast."

"I think we have to wait for daylight," Jack looked toward the windows at the front of the house, beyond which, the storm raged. "It would take you until daylight to make it to the nearest hint of civilization, if you could make it at all. It's dangerous out there. When the storm passes and we can see what we're doing, I'll fix the van and we'll get Maya to the nearest hospital. Okay?"

"He's right." Kiley was near the window to the right of the front door. "It's turning to sleet."

Right on cue Jack heard the clatter of freezing rain hitting the windows. There was no way they were getting out of there tonight. Part of him wanted to board up all the windows and doors, but he knew damn well that wouldn't keep out a ghost.

"Why me?" Johnny asked the question to the silent room as the others unrolled and arranged their respective sleeping bags.

"Why you, what?" Kiley asked, heading closer to the fireplace.

Jack touched her shoulder, and nodded at the floor in front of the couch. "Right there, close to Maya, okay?"

She saw where he pointed, nodded and moved her bag there.

"Why am I the one Gabe keeps possessing?" Johnny asked.

Kiley unzipped her bag on one side, folded back the top, then sat down in the open spot. "It must be awful," she said.

"It's..." He lowered his eyes, didn't go on. Maybe couldn't. "It is."

"Good question, though," Chris said. "I'm closer to Gabe's age. Twenty-two, he was nineteen. You're what, Johnny, twenty-seven?"

"Nine." He unrolled his sleeping bag lengthways, head near the sofa, feet toward the fireplace. Chris did the same at the foot of the sofa. And Jack unrolled his beside Kiley.

"Oh, I get it," Kiley said. "You manly men are creating a barrier around the helpless womenfolk."

Jack chose not to navigate that minefield. Instead he said, "What else do we know about Gabe?"

"He was in love," Maya said softly.

Everyone turned her way. "Hey," Johnny said. "Hey, there you are."

"How are you feeling?" Kiley asked. "How many fingers am I holding up?"

"My head hurts," she replied. "And I don't think the fingers thing is a valid medical test, but two." She sat up slowly, one hand to her head. "What happened?"

"You were heading for your car," Johnny said. "A tree fell on you."

"My car!"

"Under the tree," he said. "No way to tell how much damage."

"And the van won't start," Jack put in. "Though I'm sure I can get it going once the storm passes and I can see what I'm doing. If you need a hospital tonight, though—"

"I don't," she said. "I feel like I'm fairly okay."

"We never should've come here at night." Kiley slid her legs into the sleeping bag, still sitting up. "We should've waited until morning."

"Nothing we can do about it now," Jack said. "We're here. We just have to get through the night, and we'll be fine." He slid into his sleeping bag, jeans and all, because it would be easier to run for his life if he wasn't in his underwear. He was trying to be the strong, protective male here, but he was frankly scared shitless. Freaking ghosts, anyway. Why the hell did they have to be real?

"I'm not sure why Gabe chose you matters, Johnny," Chris said. "We have to figure out what he wants."

"All I could feel was this longing, this yearning."

"For Rosalie?" Maya asked.

He nodded. "Coupled with the frustration of her being out of reach. He can see her, but he can't touch her, can't speak to her, can't make her understand."

"So then I wonder why you were trekking through the woods in the opposite direction from where she is?" Chris asked. And when everyone looked at him, he pointed. "Rosalie is south of here. Way south. But you were hiking north, and away from the road."

"Not me. Him." Johnny was sitting up in his sleeping bag. The firelight painted his face in weird patches of orange-red light and red-brown shadow. "I couldn't sense what he was planning, but there was a plan. *Is* a plan."

"Is? Do you feel as if he's still in you, Johnny?"

He shook his head quickly. "No. No, it's all good."

"Here." She took off her necklace, a five-pointed star within a circle. It had a giant, milky stone in the center that reflected the firelight. "Wear my moonstone." Leaning down, she draped it over his head, then lowered the pendant to his chest, pulling out the neck of his T-shirt to drop it inside. "It should be touching your skin."

"Okay," he said, but Jack got the feeling his brain was no longer connecting to his voice.

"Try to get some sleep if you can, everyone. I'll take the first watch." Jack sat in a chair, instead of in the bag beside Kiley's.

"I'll take second," Chris said.

"I'll be on watch all night." Johnny slid deeper into his sleeping bag and lay down, despite his words.

Everyone settled into their respective nests as if to sleep. But nobody slept. They tossed and turned but nobody slept.

And then around midnight, Johnny got up. He leaned over the coffee table where they'd laid out everything they thought could be used as a weapon, which was stupid, because what weapon do you use on a ghost? Anyway, he leaned over and picked one up, and then he went around the sleepers and straight to the front door.

Jack sat up and started to say something, but Kiley put a hand on his shoulder with a "Shh. Let's just follow, see what this plan is, huh?"

Johnny went outside and left the door wide open behind him. He wouldn't have done that if he'd been himself. So Gabe must be piloting him again. "Good idea." He got out of his bag, grabbed his flashlight from the table, and glanced at the other items there.

"What did he take?" Maya asked, sliding off the sofa and pulling on her tall boots.

"The collapsible shovel."

CHAPTER TWELVE

hey stood around with flashlights while Johnny-slash-Gabe dug in the spot where he'd fallen before, right in front of the large pine tree. They'd tried to get him to stop, they'd tried to offer to take a turn, but he was unreachable and unstoppable.

It had turned colder. The rain had become sleet, then snow that fell in gigantic fluffy flakes that were beginning to pile up on the ground. But at least the wind had died down. Johnny's digging was slow and methodical, and then he went still for a second, and slow-mo fell right into the pit he'd been digging.

"Johnny!" Maya shouted.

"Hey!" Jack dropped into a crouch and grabbed his shoulders. "Help me get him up out of there!"

Chris reached into the hole, which was only a couple of feet deep, to try and help. But Johnny came awake in a full-blown panic, and scrambled out all at once, slipping twice on the way, and swearing a blue streak. Not like him at all. Then he stood there, staring down, and wiping his hands repeatedly across his chest.

Everyone looked into the hole where he was looking. There was a body, wrapped in clothing, caked in mud.

"Oh my God," Kiley said. "Is that....?"

"That's Grandma Nisha's coat." Jack confirmed it, but she still couldn't believe her eyes.

"Holy God."

The body was curled on one side, its head invisible in the depths of that trademark fur-trimmed hood. "So...Rosalie's mother did it? She murdered her daughter's lover, then wrapped her favorite coat around him and buried him in it? That doesn't make any sense."

"We have to call the police," Chris said. He was looking at Johnny, who was hugging himself and shivering. "Even if we have to walk to the nearest phone or cell signal."

"Agreed," Jack said.

"Yeah, I'm afraid that's not gonna work for me," someone said. Not one of them.

A tall, broad-shouldered man wearing a lined flannel jacket, his face covered in a curly white beard stood a few feet behind them. Kiley could have mistaken him for buff Santa, making a pre-Christmas Eve test run, except for the shotgun he held.

"How about we all go back inside where it's warm while I figure out which one of you is gonna go insane and murder the other four."

"Who the fuck are you?" Kiley moved as if toward him, but Jack held out an arm to keep her back.

"This is Rosalie's father. The long-lost Edward O'Reilly Cantrell," Jack said.

"*He* did it. *He* killed Gabe!" Johnny was staring at the guy, his face stricken.

"Nice guess. Now back to the cabin."

Jack nodded, sending his unspoken message to the others. Follow his lead. He'd figure something out. Kiley was damned if she knew what. He put his arm around her shoulders, gave a squeeze, and nodded at the others to precede them. Maya took Johnny by the hand and led, wanting, Kiley thought, to keep Johnny as far from that man and his gun barrel as possible. She was the one with the head injury but it was as clear to her as it was to Kiley that Johnny was the one in trouble, just then.

Chris fell in behind them, and then Jack started forward.

Kiley felt as if the gun's cold barrel were touching her bare skin, that's how aware she was of it pointing at her and Jack from behind. He could trip and fall and kill her by accident. The snow came down harder. She couldn't even see the footprints they'd made on the way out there.

She leaned toward Jack and whispered, "He only has two shots."

"No talking or you can go in the hole with Gabe."

"Why did you kill him?" she asked.

"He knocked up my daughter."

"No, sir, I did not." Johnny said it, but not in Johnny's voice. It was like butter, his accent. "You did that."

"Who the hell? What the hell?" The gunman pushed his way between Kiley and Jack and ran right through Chris, knocking him on down on the way. Maya was tugging on Johnny's arm to get him moving. There were still yards to go between them and the edge of the woods. The cabin. The van. Anything.

And then Edward caught Johnny by the shoulder and spun him around to look into his eyes. And then his own widened, and his gun arm went lax, so the rifle lowered to his side. "Gabe? How the hell...?" Then he grabbed Johnny around the neck in a head-lock and squeezed.

Jack let go of Kiley's hand and surged forward. Maya clawed at the old man's hand, then turned to pummeling his face. Jack dove, taking the rifle out of Edward's grip on his way to the ground. He landed hard, but maybe the snow cushioned his fall, because he rolled onto his back and leveled the gun on the old guy like Clint fucking Eastwood in his prime.

"Let him go, Edward."

Then the old fuck started laughing. He tightened his arm around Johnny's neck and picked his body up off the ground with the force of his squeezing. Johnny's eyes bulged. His mouth gaped in a desperate search for air.

"It's not loaded, you dumb fuck! Ahahaha!"

Jack moved around to flank him, putting Johnny out of his sites, and pulled the triggers both at once. The empty *click* echoed through the snow-silent forest. And then Jack let out this sound of pure rage, flipped the gun around and bashed the old pig in the head with it.

Edward went down like a tub of lead, and so did Johnny. Johnny crawled off to one side, and knelt, head hanging between his arms, gasping. But Edward, father of his own twin grandchildren, Sara and Kev, stayed down.

Jack dropped to his knees. "Jesus, God, did I kill him?"

"Okay, you're okay." Kiley knelt with him, reaching for the old pervert, partly aware of Maya and Chris helping Johnny, who was coughing and gasping on the ground.

She pressed her fingers into the guy's neck but didn't feel anything. Not that she knew what the hell she was doing, anyway. Then she saw blood soaking through the snowflakes as they landed on the shotgun's wooden stock, and more spreading in the snow beneath his head.

"We'll get help for him," she said. "But we have to help Johnny now. Look." She pointed at what was happening a few yards away where Johnny was up and storming back the way they'd come with Maya and Chris grabbing and cajoling him to stop.

Jack looked down at the man. "He's dead, isn't he?"

"I think, so yeah."

"We should do CPR."

"I don't think we can bring him back from that." Jack looked up at her, asking what she meant with his eyes, and then returned to scanning the body. She knew when he saw the blood in the snow under Edward O'Reilly Cantrell's head, because he gave two stuttering gasps.

She said, "Hey, I love you for being so sensitive, but this fuck raped his daughter and fathered his own grandtwins from hell. And if you hadn't done something, he'd have killed Johnny. Who's the world better off with, do you think? Some old pervert or our Johnny?"

"I don't think we get to decide that."

"Well, I hate to break it to you, but you just did. And I'd have done the same. Now let's go take care of Johnny before this asshole's noble sacrifice is for nothing. Get off your ass and move."

He got off his ass. But he'd killed a man, and Kiley didn't think he was gonna get over that anytime soon.

Finally, they arrived back where they'd been, that damn hole in the ground.

Johnny was on his knees, sobbing beside the shallow grave of Gabriel York.

The boy lay in the fetal position. His jeans had been reduced to patches of fabric here and there, revealing leather like skin and bones underneath. But the coat, Grandma Nisha's red parka, was almost perfectly preserved, if caked in earth.

"Nisha suspected what her husband was going to do. She followed him that Christmas Eve," Johnny said. "But she got here too late." He looked at them all. "Gabe wants to show us. Please join hands."

"Look, we have to go back to the cabin," Jack said. "We have to report this to the authorities."

"There is no hurry," Johnny said. "Not anymore."

Kiley nodded, dropped to her knees on one side of Johnny and took his hand. Maya took the other one, and then Chris knelt and took hers. "Come on," Kiley said, shaking her hand at Jack.

Sighing, he knelt and took her hand.

There was an immediate bolt of sizzling light, and then everything was different.

~

"I love you," Gabe said, as snowflakes fell around the two of them. They were in the park, had been skating by the light of the holiday strands that outlined the pavilion and those from the Christmas tree, twinkling in every color.

She was so beautiful as he knelt there, looking up at her. He tried to memorize her face in that moment. Her cheeks were pink with cold, her eyes sparkling, first confused, and then with dawning understanding. Was she stunned? Surprised? It was so hard to tell with Rosalie. She almost never smiled. Her eyes were filled with a sadness he'd never been able to identify and longed to erase.

He hadn't asked her yet, he realized. "M-marry me, Rosalie."

"Oh, Gabe. Oh, I... Oh. Oh." Her voice dropped an octave from first to last oh, and her head dropped with it. "I... I can't marry you. It wouldn't be fair. I'm pregnant."

He had never been so stunned in his life. "But ... but I thought that we... Who? Who?"

"It wasn't... by choice." She turned away, head down, every part of her posture ashamed.

"Someone... someone raped you? God, baby, why didn't you tell me? Or the police or your parents?"

"It was my father!" She blurted the words on a flood of emotion. Tears and sounds of pain torn from deep in her chest, from deep in her being. He knew it was the first time she'd said the words aloud. He sensed it, the power of it.

He held her in silence, because he didn't know what to say. He wanted to kill the man. He wanted to hurt Edward the way Edward had hurt Rosalie.

"He'd have killed me if I'd tried to abort. And now it's too late.

Twins, the doctor says." Then her eyes widened and she said, "He'll kill me now, for telling you."

"No, he won't, and he'll never lay a hand on you again, either. I'm taking you away from here. Tomorrow night."

"But that's Christmas Eve!"

"What better night to start our new life together?"

"But...but how, and where, and what would we—?"

"I know a place where we can go for a while, just until we figure out what to do. My uncle Sammy had a hunting cabin, way up north in the middle of nowhere. Nobody knows about it. He left it to me when he died. I'll go tonight, get it ready for the two of us. And then tomorrow night, on Christmas Eve, I'll come for you. I'll come at midnight Christmas Eve." And then he fell to one knee again. "I love you, Rosalie. Please come away with me. Please be my wife."

"I love you so much." They kissed and kissed again, and in between the kisses, and the tears, she kept saying yes.

He walked her home, stopping yards from her back door, where no one would see them together. He hid there in the woods, and watched until she was safely inside. Something cracked behind him, and he jumped, then scanned the darkness. But nothing moved. And he had things to do.

Gabe jumped into his car, and drove through the night, toward the hunting cabin hideaway. The place where they would be together. Where she would be safe.

As for the children, he would think about them later. He only knew he loved Rosalie and would do whatever it took to protect her. He thought those feelings would probably extend to her children, as well. He would be a father to them. They need never know the horrible truth.

He got to the cabin by dead of night, but it didn't matter. He knew it well. His grandfather had brought him there many times. No one else knew about it because there was no one else to know.

He found the key in the hidden niche in a log, and unlocked the door. He started up the generator, knowing how, and the lights came on as if by magic. And then he found the saw. He had a Christmas tree to cut down and decorate. And he supposed, some cleaning to do. In the morning he would find some bedding, maybe a new mattress. Maybe some dishes and cooking pans. The place wasn't bereft, there were cleaning supplies and toilet paper, a few garbage bags, and a handful of musty smelling pot holders. The furniture was permanently wrapped in slip covers and plastic. The plastic could come off. There was no bed, and only a tangle of coat hangers hung in the bedroom closets.

But he'd figure all of that out. First, the tree.

He knew just the right one.

Humming a Christmas Carol, Gabe set off into the woods, grabbing the ax from the wood pile as he went. It was snowing, and briskly cold, so the fallen leaves on the ground were coated in ice and crunched under his footsteps. The air was as cold as a whiff of straight wintergreen. His nostrils were freezing together.

He found the tree, stroked its needles, and thought of how surprised Rosalie would be. How delighted. How happy.

No wonder Rosalie never smiled, he thought.

He would pick up pinecones for decorations. There was a roll of twine underneath the kitchen sink.

"Sorry, little tree. My girl needs something to smile about. She needs Christmas." And then he chopped the tree down with about five blows of the axe. Its sap made his hand sticky as he carried the little tree back to the cabin, gathering pinecones along the way. He stopped outside the cabin's door, leaned the axe against the wall, and held the tree up to shake off the snow.

Something thudded, and he thought it sounded like a car door closing very far away. But then as he listened, a pinecone dropped from a tree and thudded into the snow, making a similar sound.

He shook his head at his nerves, then pulled the tree inside. He'd already figured out the makeshift tree stand. A mop bucket, and some twine tacked to two walls and wrapped around the trunk. It worked like a charm.

He found the twine, and used it to hang pine cones from the branches, made a paper chain from newspapers. He even found a few seashells on the window sill, and used those as well. And then he stood back to admire the tree. "I wish there were lights," he said.

"Oh, you're gonna see lights," a man's voice said, and he was just identifying that voice as Edward, Rosalie's pig of a father, when he turned and saw the axe blade descending from the corner of his eye. It embedded deep into his being and ripped him right out of his body.

He was flung across the room, but when he picked himself up, nothing hurt. And he wasn't bloody. But his body was separate from him, still lying on the floor where he'd fallen. Its head wasn't round anymore. The ax had split it clear to the nose and he had to look away from the stuff spilling out of it. Its eyes were open, but there was no one looking out through them. Because the one who used to be looking out through them had been flung across the room, he guessed.

He was dead, Gabe realized slowly. The man who had raped his own daughter had murdered him. And now who would protect Rosalie from him? Who would protect her babies?

The door flew open and there was a horrible scream.

Rosalie's mother Nisha sped to the body on the floor, fell to her knees, and then turned away sobbing and crying. "How could you? How could you do that to Gabe? My God. My God, Edward, my God!!"

Edward shook his head, walking toward her, like he'd put his hands on her shoulders and comfort her, but she pulled a handgun and pointed it at him. "Not one step," she said. "Not one." Her hands were shaking, the gun was rocking crazily in them, and she backed away as she spoke. "You—you have to leave here, do you hear me?"

"Don't be crazy. Look, it had to be done. He...he violated our Rosalie, he—"

"*You* did that." She let go of the handgun with one hand, dipping into the pocket of her oversized parka and pulling out a handful of pages covered in handwriting. "She wrote it all in her diary. I cut the pages out... I couldn't bear it being there, a permanent record of your mortal sins. Of her suffering. Of my own ignorance. But it's all here, what you did to her. How long you've been doing it."

He backed away. "She made it up—"

"I should kill you right now!" She shrieked the words at him. "Don't lie to me about my child. Go. Go, right now, before I change my mind. Leave and never set foot near me or Rosalie or her babies ever again. Vanish. Do you understand me? If you ever come back, I'll lead the police straight to the body." She held up the crumpled pages. "And I'll give them the truth in our daughter's own words."

He stared at the gun like he was thinking it over.

"I should be burying you in these woods tonight, not Gabe. Now go. Get out. Get out!" She thumbed the hammer back and lifted the barrel to aim it right between his eyes from just beyond his arm's reach, and her hand was no longer trembling.

He lowered his head, started for the door.

"No," she whispered. "No, I can't let you just walk away. I'm sorry, Edward." She stiffened her grip and squeezed the trigger, but Edward shoved her backward, so the shot went wild, and then he ran like the coward he was. He ran out the door, she stood there, still holding the gun and sobbing.

After she heard Edward's truck fade away into the night, she knelt again, her hands going to Gabe's shoulders, only they were not his shoulders anymore, he supposed. She took off her favorite coat and draped it over him, covering his poor, broken head. "I'll take care of Rosalie, Gabe. And the babies. I promise. But she can never know the truth."

Gabe cried out loud, or thought he did, from where he stood formless in the corner, he howled like the north wind. Rosalie had to know the truth. Someone had to tell her the truth. He'd promised her yesterday that he would come for her, tonight, on Christmas Eve. Her heart would be broken.

Sniffling and wiping her nose on her sleeve, Nisha pulled a blanket from the sofa onto the floor, and rolled him onto it. Then she knotted one end of the blanket and took the other end to pull his body across the floor, out the door, down the steps. She had to stop every few steps to rest, but she persisted, dragging his corpse along the driveway and slowly into the woods, stopping to tuck her favorite coat more snugly around him when bits began leaking onto the ground.

CHAPTER THIRTEEN

One by one, they let go of each other's hands, blinking themselves back to reality. Kiley looked down into the grave, feeling as if she knew the young man who was buried there.

"Edward O'Reilly Cantrell was declared dead by a judge seven years later," Jack said slowly.

"But how did Rosalie not put it together?" Maya asked. She rose and brushed the snow from her pantlegs. "Her father and her betrothed vanished on the same Christmas Eve, all those years ago."

One by one, they got to their feet.

"She didn't know it was the same night," Jack said. "Remember, according to Nisha's statement to the police, her husband left her on the twenty-first."

"The longest night," Maya whispered.

"Rosalie was probably so overwrought over Gabe's not showing up..." Kiley said, thinking aloud. "Pregnant with twins by her own father, and abandoned by the love she thought would save her?"

Chris was nodding slowly. "I wonder how long before Gabe's ghost...you know...appeared to her."

"When I was working with her, she told me she'd been seeing the ghost of her first and only love since her sixteenth birthday."

"Her birthday is in April," Johnny said. "God, she must've been devastated, all that time." His voice was his own again, but heavy with sadness and the knowledge left behind by Gabe. "I imagine that Christmas became a blur of pain for her. If her mother told her later that Edward had left on the twenty-first, Rosalie had no reason to doubt it.

"At least, not until she started seeing Gabe's ghost, all silent and sad," Kiley said.

Johnny nodded. "He can't move on."

Maya said, "And she refuses to go without him."

Everyone nodded because it felt true.

"What do we do now?" Chris asked. "We can't just leave him in the ground like this."

"We have to," Jack said. "We have to get to a phone or a cell signal and call the police in here, tell them everything that happened." And he started walking over what was becoming a path from Gabe's grave to the cabin.

"Everything?" Kiley asked, following him with the others close behind. "You tell them everything and you're either gonna wind up in a cell or a psych unit."

"I'm not going to lie to the police, Kiley."

"Did I say lie? Did anybody hear me say lie?" She looked behind her at the others, who made various expressions of not me, no way. "Look, just...minimize the ghost stuff and maximize the human stuff. We came out here looking for clues about what happened to Gabe, found his body, and Edward wanted to keep his secret so he tried to kill us."

"How did he know?" Jack asked. "How did Edward know we were coming up here?"

"I don't know."

Chris said, "We didn't tell the twins we were coming here, did we?"

"No," Jack said. We came up here as soon as we found—"

"We checked our directions at that last gas station, just before the phone-bars blinked out. That guy, that guy in the overalls."

"Ben," Chris said.

Kiley widened her eyes at him. "What is he, a friend of yours?"

"The patch on the overalls said Ben."

She shook her head, a little bit in awe of his brain. Then she looked ahead and realized they were coming up on where Edward had fallen. Where Jack had...killed him. "We should probably put a coat or something over his face, don't you think?"

Johnny said, "He doesn't deserve your fucking coat."

Then they were *in* the spot where Jack had killed the man. But the man wasn't there. Blood in the snow and a faint imprint marked the spot where Edward had been. Footprints led away through the woods, angling toward the road. And just as they all looked in that direction, they heard a motor start up, then it grew fainter as it moved away.

"Wait, he wasn't dead?" Kiley asked.

"ThankGodThankGodThankGod," Jack lowered his face into his hands for a minute, but kept whispering the same words behind them.

Kiley didn't feel she would've been anywhere near as upset over killing a child raping murderer, herself. She'd been wondering how to tactfully suggest they just bury the asshole in the woods and never mention his involvement at all.

"We have to get the hell out of here," Chris said. "We are the only people breathing who know what he did and that he's still alive. If you think he's not coming back for us—"

"Sun's up," Jack said, walking faster than before. "We'll just figure out what the asshole did to the van—"

"Wait, you think that was him, not the ghost?" Maya asked. And when he nodded, she said, "And the tree?"

"I don't know. I don't know." They emerged into the weed-filled old driveway. Chris looked toward the road. "We heard him drive off, so we have time."

"I don't think we'd better assume that we have any time at all," Kiley said. "Johnny, stay outside with Jack, watch his back while he works on the van. The rest of us will pack up our gear. But call us the second it's ready. We'll take whatever we have and leave the rest. Okay?"

Jack looked at her for a second with some kind of distracted expression, but then he shook himself and said, "Yes. Okay. Go!"

"Looks like he yanked some spark plug wires," Jack called. He straightened from under the hood and looked around. Johnny was already searching the weeds along one side of the van, so he began doing the same on the other. "He probably just whipped them. Doubt he took the time to hide 'em or—"

He jumped at sudden motion, but it was only Kiley, sleeping bags bundled in her arms. "That would be easier if you rolled them."

"We'll roll them on the road." She wrenched open the van's rear doors and hurled the bags inside, then sprinted back toward the cabin as Chris and Maya emerged, each carrying a large cooler.

"Found 'em!" Johnny came running with a handful of black wires and spark plug caps like a handful of snakes. Chris and Maya put the coolers into the back of the van and headed back into the cabin

"Great, great." Jack took the plug wires and leaned in to re-attach them. "Johnny, try to start it up."

Johnny got inside and turned the key, which was still in the switch from the night before. He tried, and the engine whirred and nothing much else.

"Hold up! I thought that might've been wrong." Jack switched the wires around. "Try again."

This time the van started. "Yes!" He slammed the hood down and turned to shout to the others, but they were already on their way, each bearing a backpack or gym bag. Johnny got out to take the oversize pack Maya was carrying. Jack got behind the wheel, and Kiley took the passenger seat. Once everyone had crowded in and slammed the doors, Jack drove forward, through the tall grass that had never been a driveway, because he couldn't back up with Maya's car under a tree behind him. He couldn't see what the ground was like, and prayed he wouldn't hit a hole or a ditch or a tree stump or...wait, there was the road, just ahead. He sent Kiley a relieved smile. "We're gonna make it."

Edward O'Reilly Cantrell stepped right out in front of them, not ten feet ahead, his white hair matted with red-black blood. He raised his shotgun up to his shoulder.

"Down!" Jack stomped the accelerator to the floor as flames flashed from both barrels. The windshield exploded.

They hit the road, Jack felt it, and turned left without being able to see. He popped up for a quick look and didn't see any sign of the murderous asshole, so he kept the pedal down. "Is everyone okay?"

They all answered yes and started to straighten up, and then the back windows exploded, too.

Maya screamed and there was blood on her arm and Johnny started swearing, then said, "It's the glass, not a bullet. You're okay, you're okay. She's okay."

One of the rear doors had flown open and was flapping in the wind as Jack drove.

He said, "Chris, can you get the door?"

Chris crawled to the back, and Jack wanted to slow down so he wouldn't bounce the kid right out onto the pavement, but he saw headlights in his rearview mirror, closing fast. "Hurry up, Chris."

Chris pulled the door closed, knotted it in place with his own belt, and scrambled closer to the front. "He's coming."

"I know."

Johnny was tending Maya's arm, cut from the exploding glass, and Kiley was refreshing her phone in hopes of getting a signal. The vehicle behind them, a pickup truck, was gaining on them. The van was not designed for speed.

"Got a bar!" Kiley yelled. "Pick up, pick up."

"Nine-one-one, what's your–"

"We are being chased and shot at by a man in a pickup truck. I'm sharing my GPS location with you now." She paused and tapped something on her screen, then returned to the call. "We are in a white van."

"We have someone in the area. Keep driving south, they will intercept you. And stay on the line be–"

Kiley frowned, looked at the phone, "What the–?"

Beep Beep Beep.

"Dropped the damn call."

"Help's on the way, though," Jack said. "You guys, pile all the equipment up against the back and stay low and way up as near the front as you can, in case he starts shooting again."

"Right!" Chris started moving stuff immediately. "More for the bullet to pass through before it gets to us."

"Go, help him," Maya told Johnny. "I'm fine, it's fine."

He'd wrapped her arm in gauze and still had his hand around it. She pressed her hand over his and nodded at him to go, so he did. And sure enough, another shotgun blast ripped their way, but it missed the van entirely, that time.

Finally, like a blessing from above, Jack heard a siren in the distance.

Edward must've heard it too, because he hit the brakes,

skidded the pickup around sideways, and then took off again in the opposite direction.

"Yes! He's gone!" Chris said.

The police car sped past them, the fellow in the passenger side giving them a thumbs up on the way by. Everyone in the van let out a whoop or cheer.

CHAPTER FOURTEEN

*I*t wasn't until nightfall, that they finally pulled into Kiley's driveway in the van. It wasn't made to seat five, but it had worked out fine. Maya had been given a CT scan, two stitches, and a clean bill of health. They'd all given statements to the police, who had accompanied them back to the site and Gabriel York's remains. There had been no sign of Edward O'Reilly Cantrell.

It was kind of automatic, all of them coming back there, to Kiley's big old spooky house. Kiley didn't mind the whole gang there, for a change. She didn't even like thinking about them all going home. Not just then.

They all went inside. They were dirty and exhausted.

The scent of pine greeted Kiley when she opened the front door. The tree lights were aglow, and there was a fire snapping happily in the fireplace. She turned around, frowning at everyone. "Who kept the fire going?"

"Who turned on the tree lights?" Jack asked. "We turned them off when we left."

She looked around the place, rolled her eyes. "Ghosts again?"

"At least they're warm, Christmas-loving ghosts." Maya had a thick bandage on her arm, and another on the back of her head, where they'd shaved a bit off her white-blond hair to stitch up the crack the tree had made. She sank onto the sofa.

"Still," Kiley said, "maybe we'd better—"

"Search the house," Jack filled in. "I'm on it."

"I'll go with." Chris clapped Jack's shoulder and the two of them went deeper into the house.

"You guys want something to drink or eat or—"

"Girl, sit down before you fall down." Maya spoke without raising her head from the back of the sofa.

"You know what? You're right." Kiley dropped into the big chair she loved best. "We have to talk to the twins, though. The cops will tell them—"

"The cops don't even know what *to* tell them," Johnny said. "They'll say that their dead grandfather killed their father and buried him in the woods, then faked his own death. It's entirely the wrong information."

"All the more reason we should prepare them with the right information," Maya said.

"Yeah, that'll be a conversation, won't it?" Kiley asked. "Your dead grandfather is alive, and he's actually your dad. He killed the guy you thought was your dad to keep him quiet about the fact that he'd raped and impregnated his own daughter, your mom."

"We can't really prove that part of it, though," Maya said softly.

"DNA could." Johnny sighed, lowering himself onto the sofa beside Maya, but not too close. "But that will be up to the twins to decide, I guess. They might not want to know."

"I might not blame them," Maya said.

Kiley pulled her phone from her jacket pocket, only then realizing she was still wearing a jacket. And it was warm, thanks to the ghost fire. She shrugged it off while tapping her phone, then let herself sink deeper into the soft chair and curled into a comfortable little ball.

Jack and Chris came downstairs and passed through the room to continue their search. Chris went straight through to the dining room. Jack paused and glanced at her, then took the plush throw from the back of the sofa, brought it to her, and laid it over her where she was curled in the chair.

She met his eyes and thanked him there. He acknowledged it. No words were needed. Then he continued on his way to the basement, where only a short time ago, they'd discovered horrors that still haunted her dreams, if not her house.

Her thumb lingered over the contact for Sara Cantrell on her phone.

And then it rang, and Sara's name lit the screen.

"Dang, I wonder if this psychic shit is contagious," she said, and tapped the answer button.

Before she could say "hello" Sara's voice stabbed her ear drum. "Did something happen? What the hell happened?"

Jerking the phone away from her ear, Kiley hit the speaker button, and cranked the volume.

"What's going on, Sara?"

"Mom's going crazy! Things are flying around the room. By themselves. Jesiz, *help!*" Kiley could hear the noise in the background, a hoarse wailing, a series of crashes.

"We're on our way. Try not to let her hurt herself."

Maya groaned and got upright.

Jack held up a hand. "I think Kiley and I can handle this one. You've been through hell. You, too, Johnny."

Johnny nodded, not even arguing. "I'll call a Lyft."

"Hey, um…why don't you guys stay here?" Kiley asked. She was grabbing her jacket off the floor, pushing her tired arms into its sleeves with no small measure of regret. "There are guest rooms to the moon and back. They're all made up because I'm a little bit OCD. Pick one." Everybody looked at her, and she said, "Or two. Or, three, because you too, Chris."

Jack frowned at her. "You sure?"

133

"Jeeze, it's three thirty in the morning. What's the point of them going home now? Besides, this way they'll all be here if we need them over at the Cantrell place." She looked at her guests and said, "I'll make Jack cook his french toast for breakfast. It's to die for."

Maya groaned at the bad pun.

"Sold," Johnny said, and he sat back down.

Chris held up his phone. "If you need us, call. Otherwise, Imma pick the best room, get a shower and some sleep."

Jack was confused by Kiley's invitation to the gang. He'd been hoping she would want *him* to stay the night, but he'd kind of envisioned them alone together. Not that he had the energy to make the most of things, but after a few hours of rest, who knew?

Kiley got behind the wheel of her old car, and he was grateful. He'd driven all the way back from that hunting cabin, after a full day with the cops. He was bleary-eyed.

She seemed wide awake.

He glanced sideways at her, noting her white knuckled grip on the steering wheel and the way she leaned slightly forward, not back against the seat. Like doing so would make the car move faster. She was doing nine miles over the limit, and he could tell she wanted to do more. They had about five minutes at the speed she was going, unless she killed them first. Maybe enough time to ask.

"So...you wanted the gang to sleep over, huh?"

She gave him a quick sideways look that felt a little sharp. "It's practically morning."

"Yeah. But none of them live far."

"Maya's injured. She shouldn't be alone overnight."

"I got the feeling she wasn't going to be," he said.

She lifted her eyebrows. "You got that, too?"

"*Hoh*, yeah. I just don't know if Johnny's aware the attraction runs both ways."

"He's oblivious," Kiley said. "Probably thinks she's out of his reach, with the age thing and...hey, wait a minute. Maybe that's why."

"Maybe what's why what?"

"Why Gabe identified with Johnny. They're both in love with women they can't reach, can't touch, can't have in some way."

Jack nodded slowly. "That's a *really* good theory."

She smiled, a little of the tension easing from her face. "They kind of work, don't they?"

"Not as well as we do," Jack said.

"Nobody works as well as we do," she shot back. Then the grin faded and her eyes looked like they were asking, who said that?

Too late, though. She'd said it.

"Here we are." She turned into the driveway just as an upstairs window exploded, raining glass down on the car. Kiley swore a blue streak, wrenching her door open at the same time. She held her arms over her head and dashed toward the front door. Jack dove out and ran behind her. The door was unlocked, so they ducked inside.

Brushing her hands through her hair in case of glass, Kiley looked around. There were crashes and loud voices coming from upstairs. She met Jack's eyes.

"We've got this," he said. "We've come this far."

They hurried upstairs, straight into the bedroom where Rosalie was sitting up in the bed, swinging her arms, kicking her legs. She latched onto an IV pole and hurled it at them, maybe because it was the only thing left to hurl. She'd cleared the nightstand. Broken glass littered the floor, a clock with its insides spilling out lay near the wall, and God only knew what she'd thrown through the window.

"Rosalie!" Jack cried, and the emotion in his voice struck

Kiley. He really cared about her. He went to the bedside and let her hands smack and claw at him. "We found Gabe. We know what happened to him. He's going to be okay now."

"Dead dead dead dead," she cried.

"Yes, but not trapped anymore. He's free now. He's free, do you hear me? Gabe is free."

"Free." A whisper. Her eyes were closed. She stopped swinging her arms. Her legs went still. "Gabe?"

Sara came from the attached bathroom, wrapping gauze around her open hand. There was blood soaking through it, over her palm.

Kev remained where he was, in the corner furthest from the bed, wide-eyed.

"He's coming for me," Rosalie said matter of factly, as she lay back on the pillows. "It's Christmas Eve and he's coming. I should get ready." Her face relaxed, and a long, relieved breath stuttered between her lips as she sank deeply into slumber or coma or whatever state she was in.

"What do you mean, Gabe is free?" Sara asked.

"Let's talk … not in here," Kiley said. "Let her rest." And she walked out of the bedroom, leaving them to follow.

They did, the twins, at least. Jack didn't and when she turned back to him, she saw him staring at a spot between himself and the bed.

"You need a minute?" she asked him.

He nodded, his gaze not moving.

"Okay, I got this." She closed the door to give him space, pretty sure he wasn't alone in there. Then she turned to the twins. "Okay, so…we went to a little cabin up north. It belonged to Gabe's uncle, who left it to Gabe when he died. It was where he planned to take your mother, when he came for her that Christmas Eve."

The twins looked at each other in stunned surprise.

Kiley took a breath and forced herself to speak the next

136

sentence. "Gabe was buried up there in the woods. We found his body."

"His...body? You found our father's body?"

"We found Gabriel York's body, yes." She cleared her throat. "And then your grandfather showed up and tried to kill us."

"That's ludicrous," Sara said. "Our grandfather is dead."

"No, he's not. Not dead and I'm really sorry to tell you this, but he's not your grandfather, either."

"I don't—"

"There's no easy way to say it. Edward O'Reilly Cantrell raped your mother, his own teenage daughter, and got her pregnant. He is your birth father. Your mom fell in love with Gabe and told him the truth. He wanted to marry her and take her away from here. And so your grandfather killed him."

Kev wobbled, then pressed a hand to the nearest wall, maybe to stay upright.

"That's *sick*," Sarah said. "And a lie. A filthy lie. How could you possibly know any of that? What, the ghosts told you? Or was it my comatose mother?"

"Gabe told us," Kiley said. "And your grandfather admitted it all. But you can prove it yourself with a DNA test. Your sperm donor murdered Gabe because Gabe knew the truth and was going to take his little girl and victim away from him. Your grandma Nisha found out what her husband had done when she read your mother's diary. So when he followed Gabe to the cabin, she followed him. But she was too late. Gabe was already dead when she arrived." She lowered her head. "Nisha told Edward to go away and never return. After he left, she wrapped Gabe's body in her favorite coat and buried him in a shallow grave in the woods. And that's where we found him. The police, who will be in touch before the night is out, if they haven't already—"

"Phone's been ringing off the hook," Sara said.

Kev sat down, right there on the floor, looking shell shocked.

"That's why he never came for her that Christmas Eve? Because he was dead? And our grandfather—our father—is still alive?"

Kiley nodded. Gabe came out of the bedroom, pulling the door gently closed behind him. "She can't see Gabe anymore. He's there, though. He can't leave her side." He sighed, looking from one twin to the other, then at Kiley. "You told them."

She nodded.

"She told us," Sara said. "But what the hell we're supposed to do with it, we still don't know." She stretched out a hand toward her brother. "C'mon, Kev, get up."

"Can we sit somewhere?" Kiley asked. "We haven't slept in thirty hours."

The twins nodded and led the way downstairs and into a sitting room with Queen Anne furniture, tufted cushions patterned in pink roses.

They all sat. Jack said, "Your mom has lingered in this state for so long because she can see Gabe. She knew he was dead and trapped here, unable to cross over until the truth of what happened to him was discovered. She refused to die without him."

"But it was our grandmother who first approached you," Kev said. "So she hasn't crossed, either?"

"I think she regretted covering up the truth. I think in death she could see more clearly what a bad decision that was. She had to make it right."

"Fine. She made it right. She led you to the...to Gabe." Sara couldn't sit. She would perch on a chair for a few seconds, they get up and pace again. "So why isn't this over? Why is all hell breaking loose now? What are we supposed to do *now*?"

"Now," Jack said, "Rosalie thinks it's Christmas Eve. She can't see Gabe's ghost, so she's once again waiting for him to arrive. I say we make it Christmas Eve. He was supposed to come for her. If she can live that night again, with the ending she wanted, I think they'll both be at peace."

"And what about our grandfather?" Sara asked. "He's still out there somewhere."

"Our concern is with the dead and dying," Jack said. "Let's let the police worry about the living. They're looking for him. They'll find him."

Sara had stopped pacing. She was fixated on a framed photo of her mother and Gabe, ice skating, their faces pensive, but clearly in love. It had been in the album before. She must have taken put it there recently. She picked it up to move it, as it probably hadn't been in the room that long ago Christmas Eve.

"They'd better find him before I do," she said.

CHAPTER FIFTEEN

"*I* think this is ridiculous, and I don't believe in any of it." Sara held up a photograph from an album, looked past it at the wall, and said, "That painting wasn't there."

For someone who didn't believe, Kiley thought she was being awfully particular about returning this room to its state on that sad Christmas-past.

The others had come to join them as soon as Jack had updated them on the plan. They were invested. They had to see it through to the end and had hurried over to help.

Kev and Chris took the painting down from the wall over the fireplace.

"There was a big wreath there," Sara said. "I think I've seen it in the attic. In fact, All Grandma Nisha's Christmas junk is up there."

"Those two words should never be uttered in the same sentence," Maya said. She was still shaken, sore, and tired.

"You sure love Christmas, for a witch," Johnny said.

The twins headed upstairs, presumably for the "Christmas junk."

"Winter Solstice," Maya corrected.

"Now you've done it," Kiley whispered, but Maya didn't even pause for a breath. "Many Christmas traditions are way pre-Christian, including the tree. I have no qualms about sharing these traditions. But they were ours, first."

Johnny listened attentively, and when she finished, he nodded exactly three times. Then he said, "Don't you think they were someone else's before they were yours?"

Maya looked at him, then at the tree standing in the corner. "Well, shit, how the hell am I supposed to be righteously indignant now? Thanks a lot, Johnny."

"You're welcome."

"A little less flirting and a little more help, huh, John?" Jack was standing on one end of the sofa. Johnny hurried over and picked up the other side, but he couldn't hide the blush in his face.

"I can't believe it's the same sofa," Kiley said, as she sent Jack a scolding look for embarrassing the two of them. Maya was blushing, too. "And the coffee tables, too. Even the fireplace screen—oh, speaking of, there was probably a fire."

The twins returned, carrying boxes. "This is not the way I'd intended to spend the evening," Sara said, lowering the oversized box to the floor.

"Wasn't what we had in mind, either, Sara," Kiley said. "But it's not about us. It's about them. They've suffered long enough, don't you think?"

She lowered her head quickly, maybe ashamed. Maybe she really did believe, and was just afraid. Maybe Kiley ought to be nicer.

~

"It's absolutely beautiful," Maya whispered.

There was a murmur of agreement. They all stood gazing at Grandma Nisha's living room. The artificial tree was an old and unconvincing one, but somehow that added to its charm. Its lights were all blue, as they had been in photos from the year of Gabe's disappearance.

They'd fluffed up the flattened plastic boughs of the old wreath as best they could, and hung it above the mantle. A tall, bone china nativity set stood below it with a bowl of plastic pine cones. Nobody liked them, but they'd been in the photos. A fire crackled warm in the fireplace.

"I think we're ready," Kiley said, nodding in approval.

"No," Kev said. "We need music. Grandma always played the same music on Christmas Eve."

"No," Sara said. "No, Kev, this might all be bullshit but it's *solemn* bullshit."

"It has to be the same," he said. He tapped his phone, waited, then tapped it again.

From a speaker somewhere, came the opening strains of *The Twelve Days of Christmas,* vocals by John Denver and…

Kiley's brows arched high. "Wait, is that…?"

"Kermit the frog," Kev said. "This is what she played, every Christmas Eve.

Sara walked away shaking her head. "This is never going to work. Even if it *was* going to work, it would never work with *that!*"

"I dunno, I think it's kind of nice," Johnny said. Maya was humming along.

"I've never heard this," Chris said. "Kermit the Frog, you say?"

Jack rolled his eyes. "I think it's time. Let's do this, okay?"

Kiley and Johnny headed upstairs to Rosalie's room, leaving the others to gather round the dining room table for a good old fashioned seance.

~

Jack sat down at one end of the table. Maya sat at the other. Chris was at Jack's right, and the twins were on the left side of the table. Pine scented candles were burning, and the Muppets had been turned down low. Kev had put one song from the album on repeat, a very slow and solemn one.

Though our minds be filled with questions,

in our hearts we'll understand,

when the river meets the almighty sea

Jack nodded, and Maya said, "Hand to hand, we cast the circle." She offered her hand to Kev and he took it, turned to his sister and repeated the words.

Sara rolled her eyes, but took his hand, and reached for Jack's. "Hand to hand we cast the circle."

Jack took Chris's hand, repeating the words, and Chris reached for Maya and completed the ring.

"This ring is made of love, and within it only love can abide. By the elements and elementals and by the powers of force and form, so mote it be." Maya nodded at the others.

"So mote it be," Jack repeated with Chris in perfect cadence. The twins came in late and awkward.

"Mote?" What the fuck is mote?" Sara asked.

"Check yourself." Maya's eyes held a warning Jack had only seen rarely. She nodded to him. "You're up."

Jack closed his eyes. "Gabe. Gabriel York. I know you're here. You're never far from Rosalie. Come to us, Gabe. We found your body. We told the police who killed you. And we'll see you get a proper burial..."

"Beside Rosalie," Sara blurted out.

Everyone opened their eyes to look at her. She shrugged. "Grandma has three plots. They were for her and Grandpa and Mom. But Gran--Edward doesn't belong there. Gabe can have his spot." She looked up toward the ceiling. "You can have it, Gabe."

"All these years we thought you were our father," Kev said,

gazing toward the staircase. "You were willing to be. Thanks for that."

Jack followed his gaze and saw Gabe there. His face and hair were clean. No paint. No mud. His clothes were clean. Grandma Nisha's coat was nowhere in sight.

"It's Christmas Eve, Gabe," Jack said. "It's time for you to keep that date with Rosalie. Long past time, don't you think?"

Gabe looked up the staircase, and then he vanished.

In Rosalie's room, Kiley hung back and watched while Johnny leaned over the bed, clasping the comatose woman's hand. He closed his eyes. "I'm a friend," he said. "I bring news from Gabe."

Her eyes popped open. Kiley gasped, then clapped a hand over her mouth so she wouldn't mess things up. Rosalie's eyes were open, and lucid, and gazing up at Johnny.

"It's Christmas Eve, Rosalie. Gabe's coming for you. Just like you both planned so long ago."

From the corner of her eye, Kiley saw someone in the doorway, and no one else was supposed to be upstairs, but as she turned to look more fully, a shadowy form streaked across the room and slammed into Johnny.

Johnny grunted and went rigid, his back arching, his arms flinging wide. And then he seemed to relax again.

"Gabe?" Rosalie whispered the name in a voice as rough as sandpaper.

"Rosalie, my girl," Johnny said in his Gabe accent. Kiley's blood all rushed to her feet and she felt dizzy. Before she could figure out what to do, though, Johnny-not-Johnny was scooping Rosalie right up out of the bed.

"Wait, wait, wait!" Kiley rushed forward, untangling tubing, lifting the IV bag from its rack and running to keep up.

Johnny-not-Johnny carried Rosalie down the stairs. On the

way, the woman pulled the IV tube from her own arm. It bled, but she didn't care. She just gazed up into Johnny's eyes with the most blissful look Kiley had ever seen.

As they reached the great room, they were backlit by the fireplace and the lights from the Christmas tree, and Kiley could see a kind of aura around Johnny, a glowing, translucent Gabriel York overlay.

She dropped the useless IV bag as she passed a table. The others came in from the dining room, Jack heading straight to her, closing an arm around her, and pulling her into his embrace.

Maya said, "Johnny? If you can hear me, Johnny, just relax. Ride it out."

"You came," Rosalie whispered.

He nodded and set her on her feet. Her legs didn't hold her weight, though, and he wound up lifting her again, and then he danced her around the room.

"You're all right," she whispered. "You're all right."

"I'll never leave you again," he said.

And from the corner, a sniffle.

Grandma Nisha, Rosalie's mother, stood watching them dance. She was all wrapped in her coat, which was just like new, but the hood was down and she was smiling. Everyone was smiling. Jack didn't know if they could see Nisha, but they could see the couple dancing, and that was enough. And then Johnny sort of sank to the floor with Rosalie in still his arms, and yet the couple were still dancing. Johnny lay on the floor beside Rosalie's body. But Rosalie and Gabe danced on.

"Ohmygod," Sara said.

Maya had tears streaming shamelessly as she fell to her knees beside Johnny, out cold on the floor, and Kiley was having a hard time holding her own back. Kev raced over, and gathered his mother up, carrying her gently to the sofa, and laying her down. Her body was lifeless, worn out, and used up.

But Rosalie was young and beautiful, dancing with her lover

to John Denver and the Muppets having the Christmas Eve they'd been denied for twenty-five years.

"Is it just me, or are we incredibly lucky to be present for this?" Kiley asked, leaning closer into Jack's embrace.

The front door crashed open. Snowy wind blasted inside, along with a large, ugly, gun-wielding maniac.

CHAPTER SIXTEEN

$\mathcal{L}$ ike a true male, Jack put himself between Kiley and the gun. In fact, his entire focus was on staying between her and Edward.

"Good, you're all here," the crazy man said.

"Grandpa?" Kev asked, and then with a look toward the sofa, his face twisted with hate. "Or should I say father?"

Johnny was still on the floor, moving his arm underneath him. Maya, had bolted to her feet when the door had burst open, but Kiley thought the sofa blocked Johnny from Edward's line of sight.

Grandma Nisha was still there, too, standing before the fire with her back to the room, wrapped in her coat and looking almost solid. The sofa's back was toward the door, so Edward couldn't see his daughter's body lying on it.

"I don't give a shit what you think of me." The tremble in his voice said otherwise.

"I think you raped our mother, you filthy pig," Sara said. "And you killed Gabe." She glanced toward where the couple had been dancing as Kiley had done, but they'd vanished.

"I was protecting my family!"

"You know what, asshole, either shoot us or get the fuck out!"

"Fine!" he said, leveling the weapon on his own daughter.

"Rosalie is dead," Kiley blurted. Anything to distract him. "She died a few minutes ago."

Edward looked at her in disbelief. "She's right there, on the sofa. See for yourself."

Frowning, he kept the gun pointed, but moved slowly forward. The door was still wide open behind him. Icy wind was still swirling inside. He moved in until he could see her lying dead.

"Rosalie?" he asked. And his voice wobbled a little. "Rosalie?"

He moved closer, reached for her, and Kev stepped into his path. "Do not lay a hand on my mother, you lecherous murderer."

"How dare you?" He lunged at Kev, but that was when the old woman in the coat turned to face him, pulled up her fur-trimmed hood, opened her mouth, and released a high-pitched, banshee-like keen. She surged toward Edward, no feet on the floor, just flew at him, and he stumbled backward, clutching his gun. She clawed at his face with her hands, and he backstepped through the door, tripped across the porch, and fell down the steps, and still she advanced. Everyone ran out onto the porch, even Johnny, as Nisha chased her husband.

Sirens screamed, but she didn't let up, driving him out into the street. As the police cars skidded to a halt and cops got out, Grandma Nisha wrapped her arms around Edward, closed her hands over his on the gun, and turned to point it directly at the police cars.

The officers started shooting and didn't stop until she let his bullet-ridden body drop to the pavement.

Then, she turned and lowered her hood and gazed back at those gathered on the porch of her home. Her mouth formed the words, I'm sorry. Then she pulled up her hood and vanished.

EPILOGUE

*I*t was the real Christmas Eve.

The food was out, the wine was chilling, and the gang was on their way. But there were still a few minutes before everyone would arrive, and Kiley intended to use them.

"I want to give you an early gift," she said.

Jack set the big platter of crackers and plant-based cheese for Maya on the table and ran to the tree like an eager kid. He hunkered down to examine the packages underneath and said, "Which one?"

Sighing, she walked over to him, holding up a red velvet ribbon with a big old-fashioned key hanging from it.

He looked at it, tilted his head.

"It's the original house key," she said. "Before I modernized the locks. I'll give you the new one, too. It's just...symbolic."

He rose from his crouched position. "You're giving me a key to the house."

"And inviting you to live here," she said. "With me." As if it wasn't clear.

He lifted his brows way up high. "You want to shack up?"

"I want to live here. But I don't want to live here alone. All that space I thought I wanted, I don't want that at all. And when you're not here, I miss you like I'd miss a limb. So move in with me."

"And what about my cabin?"

She shrugged. "You could rent it or sell it or put a yoga studio in there."

"A yoga studio, you say?" he asked, rubbing his chin.

"What you do with the cabin isn't the question, though. The question is, do you want to live here? With me?"

"Well, duh."

She lifted her eyebrows.

"What I mean to say is..." He snapped his arm around her waist, spun her into a deep dip, and bent to almost kiss her lips. "I can't think of anything I want more." And then he kissed her like the end of a golden age of Hollywood movie.

"Whoo-hoo, get a room!" Chris yelled from the doorway. They'd left it slightly open to welcome their guests. He trundled through, arms loaded. Johnny and Maya came behind him, laughing and talking, and maybe, Kiley thought, no longer trying so hard to hide the something that was going on between them. They stood close, walked close, touched often, smiled a lot.

Johnny closed the door behind them as Kiley and Jack straightened upright once more. "I'm moving in," Jack announced.

"About freaking time!" Johnny extended a hand. "Congrats, man."

Maya came in for a hug and whispered, "So, is he selling the cabin?"

"Why? Are you looking?"

Maya shrugged, and the moment passed. "There's more," Kiley said. "Get your coats off, get in here." She went to the table and poured wine for them while they tucked packages under the tree and unloaded food onto the table.

She handed a wine to Maya. Chris took one, and Johnny opted for a beer. When everyone had a drink, she said, "I think my house should be our headquarters." She held up her glass.

Nobody else did. Jack said, "That's the opposite of what you wanted."

"It's the opposite of what I *thought* I wanted," she corrected. "But after all this...look I don't like saying goodbye to you guys. I mean, I'm not saying I want you all to move in, but there are enough rooms here for you all to have a bed here any time you want or need it. The library has a separate entrance and its own bathroom. The perfect space for um... Well..." She walked over to the wall where a big object leaned, and pulled off the sheet that covered it. It was a large wooden sign that read, "Spook Central."

"I can't believe it," Maya said.

Kiley shrugged. "It's where all the ghosts show up, anyway. Besides, you're...we're kind of... family."

"Oh, man." Maya set her wine down and hugged her again, and before Kiley could extract herself, Jack, Johnny, and Chris were all hugging them, too.

"All right, all right, don't smother me," she said, laughing.

Everyone joined in her laughter. Maya grabbed her wineglass and said, "Let's get this party started."

"Here, here," Chris said. We need music."

"Got it, got it," Jack said. He reached for the remote, aimed it at the radio and tapped the button.

John Denver and the Muppets came on, full blast, Miss Piggy belting out, "Five golden rings, ba-dum-bum-bum!"

The doorbell trilled.

Everyone went silent and turned to stare at the door. Kiley linked her arm through Jack's and clutched it tight. The others followed so closely they moved toward the door as a single unit. Sending Kiley a "here goes nothing" look, Jack opened the door.

Grandma Nisha stood there all wrapped in her red parka. You

couldn't see her face, but you could feel her smile. And then she vanished and the coat fell to the floor.

Jack bent and picked it up, brought it inside, closed the door. A small package wrapped in solid red paper with a metallic gold ribbon poked out of its pocket.

He pulled it out, held it up.

Kiley said, "Open it," and then wondered why she'd whispered it.

Nodding, he brought the gift to the sofa and sat down and unwrapped the package while everyone gathered close.

Inside was a framed photo, faded with age. It was a setting Kiley remembered seeing in the albums at the house, that outdoor ice skating rink. In this shot, Nisha, Rosalie, and Gabe stood arm in arm, smiling, their eyes sparkling with joy. There had been other shots taken at this place, but none with the three of them together, and none where the subjects had been smiling.

But they were smiling now.

"This," Kiley said, "Is going to be the first thing we put in our new office."

Maya nodded in agreement. Jack lifted a glass. "Merry Christmas, Rosalie and Gabe."

"Merry Christmas, Grandma Nisha," Kiley said. And as they all tinked glasses, she added, "Don't come back, okay?" She looked around the room. "Okay?"

Continue reading for an excerpt from *Cry Wolf*, from the Brown and deLuca Series.

NEW YORK TIMES BESTSELLING AUTHOR
MAGGIE SHAYNE
A Brown and de Luca Novella
CRY WOLF

EXCERPT: CRY WOLF

"*T*his is the first year I've been allowed to come to the fair without grownups," Joshua said. He was walking along the midway, awash in carnival music and the smells of fried foods and horses.

"Are you kidding?" Toby asked. "Man, your family is nuts. I've been coming alone forever. This is like my third year." He ate the last of his cotton candy and tossed the cardboard cone into a nearby wastebasket.

"It's your *second* year," Hunter said. "And you don't come alone, you come with us." Then he shoved the teddy bear he'd just won throwing darts at balloons, into Josh's chest. "Can you fit that in your backpack?"

Toby and Chuckie elbowed each other, grinning.

"It's for my little cousin," Hunter explained as Josh took off his backpack and shoved the purple bear inside. He'd been feeling stupid for bringing one when none of the other guys had. But he'd been carrying their crap around all day, so he guessed it had come in handy. He added the bear to his collection of souvenir slurpy containers, loose change, and Chuck's inhaler.

Josh's best friends were also the three coolest guys in the sixth grade. Seventh grade, once summer vacation was over. Hunter Marks was taller than the others by a solid six inches, and he hadn't been held back even once. He was tougher than any of them. Nobody messed with Hunter, and his basketball skills had earned him the adoration of the entire middle school. Good genes, Josh thought. Toby Gaye took a lot of ribbing for his last name, but he was funny as heck, and that seemed to outweigh it. He was popular by virtue of being the class clown. Chuckie Barnes was the smallest one. He looked like that skinny baby rooster on the cartoons, Foghorn Leghorn's son, right down to the wire-rimmed glasses. His frequent bouts of asthma and scrawny physique would've made him bully bait if he hadn't been part of Hunter and Toby's inner circle.

And now, they'd sort of pulled Josh into their gang. He guessed that made him one of the cool guys now, too. He walked a little taller. After some crazy lady had tried to shoot people at his big brother's graduation party, Josh's popularity among his peers had shot through the roof. And he was glad. His mother being in a nuthouse had been his previous claim to fame. A sniper at a grad party was much cooler. His status, when he entered the seventh grade in a few weeks, was going to be way better than before. And it was about time.

Hitching his backpack up on his shoulders, he nodded toward the scariest ride on the entire midway, the Raptor, and said, "You guys want to go again?"

Each of the guys dug into their pockets to pull out what remained of their ride tickets. Toby had seven, just enough to get on The Raptor one more time. But Hunter was down to two, and Chuck didn't have any.

Josh headed over to the ticket stand, dragged a crumpled twenty-dollar bill out of his pocket, and shoved it through the opening in the plexiglass. A small lady with a chubby hand slid a flat sheet of tickets back out to him, and he started tearing them into strips along the perforations as he rejoined the group, then handed them around.

"Dude, how much money you got on you, anyway?" Hunter asked.

Josh shrugged and Toby said, "Plenty. His parents are like loaded or something. His mom's famous."

"She's not my—I mean, yeah, she *is* kind of famous." They were talking about Rachel, of course, who was not his mother. And Uncle Mason who wasn't his father. But they all lived together, like a real family, so it was close enough. He felt a little guilty about not correcting his friends. But on the other hand, if his friends were starting to forget who his real mother was, then that was a good thing for him, wasn't it?

And his real mom would never know. Right?

The guys took the tickets he gave them. There were three left over, and probably not a ride in the entire park that only took three. Josh looked around, saw a mom with a little kid about four, so he stepped into her path and held them out to her. "You can have these if you want. We're on our last ride for the day anyhow."

She took them and was still looking at him with raised eyebrows when he and the guys walked away to get in line for another round on the Raptor.

"After this, I gotta go," Josh said with a look at his phone. "My brother's picking me up at eight."

"Dude, you could *walk* home from here!" Hunter sounded as if that was a far better option. "Why's he gotta pick you up?"

He was right, of course, but the walk home was two miles over a dirt road that skirted the reservoir on one side and the woods on the other. Seasonal use only. Nobody else on it even in the summer. He hadn't even argued when Uncle Mason had told him that he had to ride home with Jeremy. The idea of walking home that way, after everything that had happened, scared the crap out of him.

Chuck elbowed Hunter. "You've seen his brother's car, though. Who *wouldn't* rather ride in that than walk home?"

The other guys nodded, saving Josh once again from having to explain something that would've been embarrassing. He was still a little bit afraid of the dark, and of long walks on deserted stretches of road in the middle of nowhere. But he didn't want to have to explain all that.

Chuckie grinned at him though, and Josh got the feeling he knew the truth. He smiled back, grateful.

The line moved fast, and the four boys got a car to themselves on one of the four-car pendulums that revolved as they swung higher and higher and higher, maxing out so high they were momentarily suspended upside down and weightless, held in their seats only by the safety bar and each boy's own death grip on it.

It was over way too fast. Josh was proud that he hadn't yelled even once. None of the guys had. But he was a little unsteady on his feet as they got off the ride and headed back onto the midway.

Then he heard a familiar bark—well, you know, the snuffly sound bulldogs call a bark—and looked up to see Myrtle and Hugo galloping toward him. The older blind bulldog, Myrtle, kept her side pressed to the puppy's side the entire way. Hugo was like her seeing-eye pup.

"Aw, dude, cool dogs," Hunter said when Myrtle bashed her iron skull into Josh's shin.

Josh crouched down, petting them both. "Hey, Myrtle, meet the guys. Guys, this is Myrtle. She's blind but she gets around great. And the pup is Hugo."

The guys bent to pet the dogs, too, and Jeremy, who was right behind the dogs, said, "Hey guys. Good day?"

They all straightened, maybe standing a little taller in the presence of Josh's big brother, Jeremy, who was far cooler than any of them by virtue of his advanced age, recent graduation, and classic ride.

"The best," Toby said.

"It was all right," Hunter said at the same time.

Chuckie stayed crouched, petting the dogs, talking to them like they were people.

"Any of you guys need a ride home?" Jeremy asked.

"We brought our bikes," Hunter said.

"Okay, that's cool. You ready, Josh?"

"Yep. See you guys. C'mon, Myrt."

Myrt abandoned Hugo to press herself against Josh's leg and they wound their way back to the parking lot and climbed into Jeremy's Iroc Z. Jere revved the motor a little, showing off for the guys while he waited for traffic to clear so he could pull out and to the left. A quarter mile later, he took a right at the stoplight, and kept going until the pavement ended, and the woods began on the left, the reservoir's sloping shore on the right.

Two miles up on the left was where they lived in a giant camper with Aunt Rachel and Uncle Mason. His friends were right about Rachel. She was loaded, and so after the firebug had torched her house, she'd picked out the biggest, fanciest camper he'd ever seen. It had four slide-out sections, a satellite dish, three TVs, and a patio. It sat on the front lawn about fifty yards from the house, which was in the process of being rebuilt.

It was pretty cool how they'd all sat down together, throwing out ideas while Uncle Mason sketched pictures and Aunt Rachel took notes. She said this time, the house was gonna be *their* dream home, not just hers, because they were all living there together from now on.

He guessed that meant she and Uncle Mace were official. And he was glad.

Josh's room was gonna be a gamer's paradise. Jeremy was getting an apartment over the garage, so he would have his own space during breaks from college, which started in just a couple of weeks. Right now their dream house was just a big empty shell, but they'd only been working on it just over a month.

It was August 1st, and life was changing. Life had been changing for him and Jeremy for a couple of years now, but this time, he thought it was changing into something really awesome. And it was about time, too.

Jere parked the car near the camper and cut the motor. Josh opened his door, and the puppy dove out of the car and stood on the ground barking like mad. Josh helped Myrtle out, picking her right up and then setting her on the ground. "Jere, I think she's getting lighter." Then he frowned. "And look, her neck rolls aren't covering up her collar anymore."

"Shh. Don't let Rachel hear you say that or—"

"Don't let Rachel hear you say what?" Rachel said, coming out the camper's little door and dropping into a crouch as Myrtle raced toward her. She caught the dog's face in her hands before she got her shins bashed. Good trick, Josh thought.

"That Myrtle's losing some of her chub," he told her. "I guess Dr. Clive was right." Josh noticed Jeremy wincing and closing his eyes.

Rachel frowned. "Dr. Clive was *not* right," she said. "Myrtle isn't losing weight. She's in perfect shape, and has been all along. Cutting out the tiny little tastes we feed her from our dinner plates—"

"And lunch plates," Jeremy said, "and breakfast plates, and bedtime snacks, and cheese sticks. Don't forget the cheese sticks."

"—hasn't made one bit of difference," Rachel continued, after sending Jeremy a lovingly withering glare. "Because we haven't been giving her enough to *make* a difference. She wasn't overweight. That vet is full of shi...blue mud."

"Right. I hear a lot of Cornell-educated vets are," Jeremy added a smile, then before Rachel could respond, said, "Yo, Josh, get your crap outta my car, huh?"

Josh turned back toward the car, but Rachel was still talking. "Myrtle is just the right size for a big-boned bulldog," she said, rubbing Myrt's ears just the way she liked best. "Aren't you, Myrt? Yes, you are."

The bulldog wiggled her butt, because she didn't have a tail. Just a curly little stub on her backside. Although, Josh thought that curly stub was protruding from her rump more than before. Yeah, she had definitely lost weight.

He reached into Jeremy's car, picked his backpack up from the seat, and then said, "Aw, crap!" Rachel and Jeremy both turned his way, waiting for the rest.

"I forgot, I've got all the guys' stuff in my backpack."

"Anything that can't wait until tomorrow?" Rachel asked. Josh pulled out Chuckie's inhaler, held it up, and she said, "Nope, guess not."

"I'll take him, Aunt Rache," Jeremy offered. "If we hurry, we can catch them before they even get home."

"Thanks Jeremy." Rachel clasped her hands near her chin and batted her eyes. "You're so selfless."

"Yeah, and you love driving your car anywhere for any reason," Josh added.

"You reap most of the benefits of that, squirt. Hop in."

"Make it quick," Rachel said. "And by quick, I mean keeping to the speed limit, Jere. You know, within reason."

He sent her a nod and got behind the wheel. Josh buckled up, and the car headed right back the way it had come from, rumbling and growling to the end of their road and then left through the village.

"So who lives closest?" Jere asked.

"Hunter. The next road on the right." The other guys lived farther along the main drag, Chuckie on the left, and Toby a little farther, on a dirt side road not unlike Josh's own.

Jeremy turned onto Hunter's road. "How far up?"

"Not far. Top of the hill and then around a sharp curve, and then—wait, wait. Jeremy stop!"

Jere hit the brakes right in the middle of the road and sent

Josh his patented WTF look, but Josh was already trying to open the door, and then he finally did and got out and ran to the bike he'd spotted lying on its side in the ditch. He scrambled down to it, his feet splashing into the water that ran in the bottom. "It's Hunter's bike!"

"Holy crap." Jeremy was out of the car, too, looking left and right, and shouting, "Hunter! Hunter, where the heck are you?"

Josh started to reach for the bike to pull it out of the mud, but he stopped when he saw what looked like blood on the handlebar. "Jere?"

His big bro was right behind him by then. "Don't touch it, Josh. He probably tried some BMX move or something and crashed. Probably limped home for a Band-Aid." He was pulling out his phone, and a second later, said, "What's his number?"

"I have it on my phone." Josh was trembling as he pulled his phone out of his pocket, scrolled to Hunter's entry and tapped the button to call his landline. The water was starting to seep into his sneakers. Mrs. Marks picked up on the second ring.

"Just ask if he's there," Jere whispered. "Don't scare her. We don't know if there's a reason to yet."

Nodding in a jerky motion, Josh said, "Hey, Miz Marks, it's Josh. Is Hunter home?"

"No, but I expect him soon. I told him before dark, so he should be here any minute. Weren't you at the fair with him?"

"Uh, yeah, but I went home and realized he left some stuff in my backpack."

"Oh, well, did you try texting him?"

"I didn't uh...didn't think of that. Thanks, Miz Marks." He ended the call, and looked up at Jeremy, who was already making a call of his own, and Josh hoped it was to Uncle Mason. Jere put his phone on speaker, and held it between the two of them.

While it rang, Jere said, "Hunter's probably still walking. Maybe he crashed his bike within the last few minutes, and he just hasn't made it home yet."

"It's not that far," Josh said, looking up the hill. He could see the beginning of the curve. Hunter's house was just the other side of it.

"Hey, Jere, what's up?" Uncle Mason's voice came from the phone speaker. Just hearing it made Josh feel a little better.

Jere nodded at him, a sort of it's-gonna-be-okay kind of nod, and said, "Hey, Uncle Mace. Um, Josh's friend Hunter was riding his bike home from the fair, last we knew. But we just found his bike in a ditch down the road from his house, and his mom says he's not home yet."

"Where's Josh? Are you safe?"

"I'm right here, Uncle Mace. We're fine."

"We're by the bike now," Jeremy said. "Right where we found it."

"Okay, stay there for now, but get in the car and lock it. Don't touch the bike. Does Hunter have a cell?" Uncle Mason asked.

"Just an iPod, but he can text with it," Josh said. "Uncle Mason, there's blood on the handlebar." He hated how hard his voice was shaking.

"I'm on my way, Josh. I'm gonna be right there. Five minutes. Get in the car and lock it, just to be on the safe side. Anyone besides me shows up, you just drive away, okay?"

"We'll drive up and down the road," Jeremy said. "See if we spot him walking or..." He shot a quick look at Josh. "...or anything."

"Okay. Do that. I'll be there soon."

Jeremy pocketed his phone and said, "Come on, let's get back in the car, kiddo."

But Josh had turned to look back at the bike in the ditch and kind of got stuck there. He couldn't even blink. "It's like we're contagious," he said.

"What do you mean?" Standing right behind him, Jeremy dropped his hand on Josh's shoulder. He had big hands all of the sudden, Josh realized. His hands were grown-up hands. When had that happened?

"It's like we've got some kind of curse on us or something, and now it's spreading to our friends. I've only been hanging out with Hunter for a month, and it's already got him."

"Aw come on, Josh." Jere tugged on his shoulder until he turned Josh around. "You know there's no curse. We've had some bad luck, that's all. This is probably nothing. Hunter's probably fine, prob'ly knocked a tooth out on his handlebar and ran home crying."

"Not Hunter. Hunter doesn't cry." Josh looked up at his brother and said, "Something bad happened to him, Jere. I feel it, right here." He pressed a fist into his belly and tried to keep breathing past the knot in his throat. "And I don't know how, but I think it's because of us."

"Shoot, you're starting to act like you're the one with NFP."

His reference to Aunt Rachel's gift, which she called NFP for not effing psychic, made Josh smile, and his heart felt a little bit lighter.

Cry Wolf is now available!

ALSO BY MAGGIE SHAYNE

Fatal Fixer Upper

The Secrets of Shadow Falls
Killing Me Softly
Kill Me Again
Kiss Me, Kill Me

Other Suspense Titles
The Gingerbread Man
Sleep with the Lights On
Wake to Darkness
Dream of Danger
Innocent Prey
Deadly Obsession
Cry Wolf
Girl Blue

ABOUT THE AUTHOR

New York Times bestselling author Maggie Shayne has published more than 50 novels and 23 novellas. She has written for 7 publishers and 2 soap operas, has racked up 15 Rita Award nominations and actually, finally, won the damn thing in 2005.

Maggie lives in a beautiful, century old, happily haunted farmhouse named "Serenity" in the wildest wilds of Cortland County, NY, with her soul-mate, Lance. They share a pair of English Mastiffs, Dozer & Daisy, and a little English Bulldog, Niblet, and the wise guardian and guru of them all, the feline Glory, who keeps the dogs firmly in their places. Maggie's a Wiccan high priestess (legal clergy even) and an avid follower of the Law of Attraction.

Find Maggie at http://maggieshayne.com

facebook.com/maggieshayneauthor
twitter.com#!/maggieshayne
instagram.com/maggieshayne
bookbub.com/authors/maggie-shayne

CPSIA information can be obtained
at www.ICGtesting.com
Printed in the USA
LVHW032147220423
745094LV00012B/175